AIDEN SHAW'S ~~PENIS~~

& Other Stories of Censorship From Around the World

AIDEN SHAW'S PENIS

& Other Stories of
Censorship From
Around the World

TWENTY SEVEN

First edition published in 2021 by Imprint Twenty Seven,
an imprint of Nobrow Ltd. 27 Westgate Street, London, E8 3RL.

1 3 5 7 9 10 8 6 4 2

Design & Typesetting by Bia Melo
Copyedited by Vimbai Shire

Printed and bound by Ozgraf, Poland
on FSC® certified paper.

ISBN: 978-1-910620-81-6

www.imprint27.com
www.nobrow.net

CONTENTS

FOREWORD

Coco Khan

When Nobrow asked me to join the judging panel – to help select this collection of short writings from new voices on the theme of The Censor – I could never have guessed the scale of ambition, diversity of style and richness of voice that I would come to read. I admit that was foolish of me. After all, censorship is not just a matter for artists and agitators, reactionaries and revolutionaries, but for every single person daring to speak, act or, indeed, exist publicly. Where there is expression, there is always the possibility of censorship, and in our era of tech-enabled mass-communication where truly 'private' space is diminishing at a rate of knots, there is a hell of a lot of censorship around.

What this collection does is interrogate that censorship and those who enforce it – The Censors – in every direction.

It covers the 'how' of censorship: the methods used by censors to ensure it occurs. In the title story, Ali Said's memoir piece 'Aidan Shaw's Penis', we meet the officials in the UAE whose job is to preserve the moral purity of the nation by quite literally blacking out material they deem inappropriate. The impact of their work is elegantly woven between vignettes from Said's own life, which is filled with other kinds of censors – be they the citizens who facilitate the official work through their own moral policing, or Said himself, denying and obscuring the truth of his own sexuality through self-censorship.

That sticky relationship between those in official power and those who collaborate with them is a recurring theme in this collection, whether it is in Fernando A. Torres' poetic retelling of a student protest levied at General Pinochet; the parents in Mitra Teymoorian's 'Three Acts from a Woman's Life', whose desire for respectability yields tragic results; or in Kiki Gonglewski's imaginative 'Vestiges', which depicts an eco-fascist dystopia where expression through objects is punished under the guise of sustainability. Elsewhere, Catherine Rudolph's sharply written 'Fortress' explores the power held by authors to manipulate truth, and write out uncomfortable truths such as white privilege; and Michael Harris Cohen's piece of historical fiction, 'Cuttings', juxtaposes the determination of a young Heinrich Heine (whose works were banned), and the dedication of a young Jacob Grimm (who faced the same) against the devotion of the censors who blind themselves in service.

But it is the 'why' of censorship – the human motivations that uphold these power dynamics – that this collection excels with. In Selma Carvalho's exquisite 'Penguin' the act of self-censorship in the setting of a patriarchal, morally conservative society is not to be complicit but to survive; while Nathan Alling Long's example of magical realism, 'The Song Bird', explores domestic relationships, where the sustained silencing of women's expression is tantamount to abuse, and a exacts a terrible price on the need to be desired.

Naturally, as in real life, the 'hows' and the 'whys' of the censors – who have often been censored themselves – are complex and intricate, and the authors kick against the all-too-easy assumption that censorship is innately bad, and censors regressive. Mubanga Kalimamukwento's 'Reflections' explores the capacity for the censors to change, and how love and grief can break through the moral 'good-bad' demarcations that censorship requires. Deborah Green's raw and powerful exploration of 'shame' from her perspective as a sex worker discusses its necessity and function in society, as well as its misuse. And in Timi Odueso's 'The Many Lives of Denola', we again see how stories told often serve the teller, but we also see how that is a vital instrument in sharing wisdom, sharing knowledge, and just having a bit of damn fun.

If I may, I would like to take a moment to note the diversity of this collection – not just in terms of the authors, who are mixed across age, race, gender and nationality – but in tone and style too. This collection runs the gamut of emotions (prepare to laugh! cry! squirm! and scream!), and it has fun with form, whether it's in Said's use of third person or how Stephanie Wilderspin's 'Refracted' shows the reader the thoughts the narrator censors while living with a mental illness in a society that demonises it.

Indeed, if this final compilation (as well as the many other excellent pieces Nobrow received from around the world as part of the competition) tells us anything, it's that censorship is as much a part of the human condition as those other universal experiences which bind us: birth, love, death, and our need for purpose. It is the matter of context, degree and application of the censorship we each experience that is the battleground. And sometimes, it is just as the playground retort says. Who are the Censors? Well, it takes one to know one.

PENGUIN

Selma Carvalho

first meet Penguin just as I'm sliding out of a bus, which has skidded off the XBR Bridge and landed on the salt flats below. I'm squirming my way out of a shattered glass window, its shards strewn all around me, when I see him standing there. A beautiful Emperor, he is about four feet tall, fitted out with a sleek, waterproof coat and an exquisite white, downy plumage covering all of what I suppose you'd call his chest.

'You're a long way from home,' I say, ingenuously.

He just stares at me. He spreads out his flippered wings like a broken-hearted Christ about to preach.

'What are you doing?' I yell, bearing on my forearms

and edging my way out.

'I'm lost,' he says. 'I'm trying to cool myself.'

Then he is gone.

Penguin is a migratory bird.

*

A week later I'm at the XBR Pharmacy and Penguin is standing there in a corner, shuffling his feet and nodding his beaked head. I tug at a pregnancy test, which they keep hidden from public view, wedged between the cotton wool and vitamins. The entire spectrum of a woman's life can be found in a pharmacy aisle: sanitary towels, pregnancy tests, folic acid, breast pumps, and menopause supplements. There you have it. In the desert a woman's body pleasures a man, it gives of itself to him, it spirals around him, and then vanishes into him.

I ignore Penguin and walk over to the cash counter. The pharmacist, a jowly, balding man, is busy with another customer, but eventually, he half-looks in my direction. I take this as my cue to approach him. I hand him the pregnancy test. His hand trembles as he takes the box and briefly grazes mine. His body stiffens.

'You married?'

His voice is hard, his eyes ever watchful over the lives of others. 'It's for a friend,' I offer, by way of explanation.

He opens the till and places the money in it. He owes me some change, but he puts his hand in his white coat and fishes out a lollipop instead. He pops it into his mouth and sucks on it real hard, his head cocked to one side, his lips locked in an imbecilic smile.

'You want lollipop?' he asks, his hand drumming the counter-top. An old-fashioned telephone rings. He answers it, weaving his fingers through its spiral tentacle. It's something about reporting statistics to the Ministry of Health.

I shove the pregnancy test into my bag. The man laughs as I run out the door.

'He's robbed you,' Penguin says, following me out of the pharmacy, heaving and puffing, trying to keep up. His waddle is infuriating, and it slows me down.

'So?'

'Aren't you angry? Shouldn't you have insisted on the money?'

'Angry? I'm a woman, living on my own, buying a pregnancy test. Do you think I'm in a position to argue with a horny man in a white coat?'

We walk in silence, Penguin and I. His black coat has grains of fine sand stuck to it, which he tries to brush off with his much-too-long beak, but the coat has lost its lustre. That's what happens when you get stranded in a desert. The sand slips into your consciousness. You lose yourself in it. You let the sand bury you alive.

'What do you want it to be? The test, I mean,' Penguin interrupts my thoughts.

'I'm terrified, you idiot. What do you think I want it

to be?'

'You want this.'

'Why would I want this?'

'Because you want to belong. All your life you've never belonged.'

'How do you know this about me?'

'I'm lost and I can see it – this sense of being lost – in others.'

Penguin looks at me sideways. He seems sage with his air of superiority, as if dispensing advice to single women walking along bare roads is his new-found mission.

I see a man walking towards us. I know the man, N the fishmonger, from the souk near my flat. N always has his sleeves folded, his vest smeared with blood, his hairy chest smelling of tailfin, his large hands gutting and scaling and slapping fish. Sometimes I catch N touching himself when he is alone in that shop. N lives in the bachelor accommodation at the back of the souk, which he shares with six other men. The desert doesn't allow N to bring over his family; the desert has strict rules about who can bring their family over. Sometimes N pulls out a picture from his wallet and shows it to me. It's of a young man – his son. He hasn't seen his son in ten years. N is an undocumented worker, a fugitive from the Ministry of Immigration, and can't travel to his home country. I don't want to think of N as a pervert. I like to think N imagines his faceless wife when he's touching himself. That hairy bastard's only crime is not earning enough to bring his family over. The desert swallows us all up in its sandstorms, gusting at great speed until everything on the windward side is a grainy blur.

I touch my stomach gently and quicken my pace. I'm so afraid N will see Penguin, but I needn't worry. In the desert we get used to hiding ourselves.

Penguin is a flightless bird.

*

On the corner of XBR Road I turn left, walking towards the colony of flats which house the worker-ants that sail in from the islands to churn the wheels of commerce and industry. The Ministry of Immigration has a record of each one of them. I begin climbing the steps to my flat. The box-like elevator, installed as an afterthought, has broken down once again. Z the watchman appears at the mouth of the stairwell, solicitous and fawning.

'I'll get it fixed by evening,' he says. His beard is dyed a fiery red, his body massaged with herbal oils, his skullcap off-kilter, and in his hands rosary beads to propitiate the Almighty.

I nod, knowing full well Z will fall short of expectations. But it is good to let the old man feel like his word means something around here.

I open the door to my flat. The ceiling fan creaks miserably, coaxing itself to recycle hot air. Penguin stands by the large sliding windows looking on to the balcony. Oh, he'll be hot today. He'll have to spend the entire day with his wings outstretched.

'Don't you have air conditioning?'

'I do, but I don't want to waste it on you.'

'Suit yourself,' he says.

I go into the bathroom, relieved that Penguin won't follow me there. I sit on the ceramic pot and pee on the plastic pregnancy stick. Then, while I wait for the future to reveal itself, I notice the cracks running across the wall.

Penguin comes in just then; I must have left the door ajar.

'Well?' he asks, tapping his comically small feet.

I look at the bathroom floor, the black-and-white tiles bobbing in front of me. That's when I decide Penguin must die.

I walk to the bathtub and turn on the cold-water tap. It is filthy, the tub, coated with dried sea-salt, its steel fittings rusted, its white surface rimmed brown. It seems incongruous to have a tub in a bathroom which, for most of the day, has no water. But the older buildings have bathtubs installed, because the architect who had drawn up the plans, in his post-colonial egalitarianism, thought everyone should have one and because the owner, newly rich, alluded to pretentions of modernity.

A drizzle of muddy water fills the tub halfway up. I lure Penguin into the tub. I kneel beside the tub and wrap my fingers around his thick, rubbery, feathered neck, tightening my grip until he splutters, gags and chokes; his webbed feet wildly splashing about in the cold water. It's only when his eyes start to bulge and he turns somewhat grey that I relent and afford him an executioner's reprieve. I stand up, dripping wet, and walk back into the hall, leaving a trail of water droplets on the threadbare carpet.

Penguin follows me in there.

'What are you going to do?' Penguin asks, shaking the water off his rubber coat.

'I don't know. What will the Ministry of Public Morality have to say about this mess?'

'Are you going to tell your lover?'

'I suppose.'

I open the sliding glass windows and step onto the balcony. The sun is hot. In the desert the sun is like this: always hot and direct. It never dapples gently onto rooftops. It blazes into houses uninvited and unwelcome.

I think of the countless times H and I have stood on this very balcony, looking at the vastness of the city beyond, the flat-roofed buildings huddled together, the bakeries, the grocers, the butcheries, the textile shops, the newly imported cars, and a little further off in the distance, the all-seeing, all-knowing ministries.

I have lived in the desert for twenty years, the daughter of workers who travelled from the islands. When they returned to the islands, exhausted and spent, they were replaced by another set of transients. I know every hard turn, every shop and every traffic stop in this city. Yet, the city does not know me; not in any way that acknowledges my existence, legitimises it, welcomes it and makes it visible. I am a blur on the periphery of this city's consciousness; a decimal point on a pay cheque, a measurable unit of production, a statistic, a casualty of sweaty ambition.

A week ago, I'd watched a flogging outside the Ministry of Public Morality. I don't know what it was for; it really doesn't matter. The real pain isn't inflicted by the hide whip, it is the humiliation of the lashes seared into the back; those marks stay forever. The world is always quieter after a flogging. A sepulchral stillness is the sign of people subdued. It takes a lot to subdue people, though. People are hopelessly optimistic, believing always the human heart will yield to forgiveness, mercy, empathy and justice. Eventually, their backs are broken, and they fall in line.

Penguin stands beside me; this flightless, aquatic bird with its overbrushed coat. I pull him up on to the ledge. Perched precariously, Penguin looks at me, and I can see the fear clouding his eyes. I don't want Penguin's fear. So, I push him over the edge. But there must have been a little flight in his wings because he lands safely on the ground and pads his way back to the flat.

Penguin can survive for long periods under water.

*

I sleep with H for a month and don't say anything. I think of the baby growing inside me when I pass by N's fish shop, and the smell of fish makes the puke ride up. I think about the baby's reptilian existence, submerged in its watery world. What if it never formed beyond its reptilian phase? It is only when I can't button my jeans that I decide to tell H.

H is sitting on the brown, bobbled fabric sofa my parents bought in the seventies, when those sofas were fashionable, and my parents' newly acquired bourgeois aspirations made them buy things they thought were trendy.

'What about my whisky soda?' H asks.

'I have whisky, but I don't have any soda,' I reply from the kitchen.

'How come? You know I take my whisky with soda.'

'I've been drinking the soda myself, quite a lot.'

If H detects an edge to my voice, he doesn't let on.

I hand H a glass with amber liquid and two floating ice cubes. He takes the glass and pulls me down on to the sofa.

'Have you heard about the temple desecrations on the island?' he asks.

H likes to talk a lot about the islands, about imagined slights to the purity of his heritage. H is fiercely nationalist. He's carrying a lot of anger within him about how the islands are changing. H wants the islands to be preserved in a time capsule, so that when he visits them, his sense of self is reaffirmed. H is one of the lucky ones. He can afford to return to the islands for a holiday. He works at an oil refinery. He earns enough to live in a sea-facing bungalow, with his wife and two kids. He can drive around at night without fear of being stopped by the police and asked for proof of identity. Poor H, you miserable bastard; lucky enough to have your wife with you, just not lucky enough to be in love with her.

H speaks in short bursts, building up momentum as he goes along. Usually, I humour him, but today the room is hot and airless, and filled with my impatience.

'I'm pregnant,' I say.

From where I'm standing at the window, I can see the Ministry of Public Morality, its dome-shaped roof flattened against the evening sky. Within its vertebrae of cold blank walls sit men who lay down the laws of the desert; men who've survived sandstorms, and now know what's best for everyone. If I think about the horrors of the world – murder, rape, hunger, war, deprivation – they are unbearable. Is it so terrible then to live here in the desert where fates are manoeuvred, where we've begun to believe that if we behave a certain way no harm can come to us, and if we keep our heads down and never ask questions then we can lead a good life? Sometimes, I imagine different versions of myself, and then believe I'm living the best version possible. The Ministry of Public Morality tells us the worst of ourselves lives in the language of protest and dissidence. The eclipse of the self by the state is easy; self-censure is the cruellest death of all, but the state exalts the body in salutary stories. Eventually, H asks, 'What will you do?'

I shrug.

'I can arrange for you to have the whole thing erased,' he suggests.

'Erasure of me is what history is all about.'

'Look here, the penalty for keeping it is death. They'll take care of the baby but they'll flog you to death.'

I look at him, my heart atremble, its beat a thudding echo. I wonder how he'd never thought about the illegality of our affair, the consequence of which is also death. But the heart is a poor conjugator of illegalities; the heart is a Minotaur spiralled in a maze, growing braver with its own delusions. I lay my head on his shoulder, knowing it will be for the last time. We sit in silence until the vortex of this violence overwhelms us, making landfall with the veiny wings of our illicit past.

'I've got to go, the wife is at home.'

I see only the back of him now, as he makes his way to the door, his body tightly wound on his powerful legs.

Penguin protects his mate's egg by keeping it warm on his feet. He spends the winter on land protecting his unborn child.

*

Late in the night, Penguin sneaks into my bed.
In the near distance, I can hear N the fishmonger

talking about his son, about sending his son off to a faraway land where the cities are freer. In the desert, the night is like this: it's cold and very still. It distils sound and thought, clarifies it, and carries it to distant realms.

I put my arms around Penguin and hold him close. We both know what we have to do to survive. We are all resurrected in our children; resurrections are feathered little things webbing futures, flapping frantically in hopeful arcs across humanity.

* * *

CUTTINGS

Michael Harris Cohen

I

ometimes Herr Weller believes it is the words that have robbed his sight. Not the strain of reading, but the words themselves. They swallow light and shroud his vision with darkness. Or the letters scramble like insects on the paper, running from eyes and pen. He must press his nose almost to the page to catch them. He's come to despise the smells of paper and ink.

Still, he works through the night. Though it hardly matters – night ... day – his lamp turned up full to contest the gloom.

He wonders at all the thoughts his mind has been forced to ingest. He cannot choose. Manuscripts are delivered, and range from poetry to botany to history. Everything written must be read and weighed for the seeds of revolt against the Prussian state. So many worlds traveled from Herr Weller's narrow desk. Yet, when he sets aside pages and moves to the next, he hardly remembers a jot of what he's read.

Where do these things go, he wonders. There is no excretory process for the mind. *Where do these things go?*

*

Morning walks used to clear Herr Weller's head. He remembers the wonder of the fog from the mountains censoring the tower of the church, the entirety of the castle, in a billowy haze. The town would vanish, then reappear as the sun rose and burned off the mist. At home, he'd read and work and wake and walk and work, and so the years passed until his world began to dim.

At first he thought the sun was rising later and later. Now he knows his world will disappear, piece by piece. Forever. He walks in perpetual dusk, his cane feeling for missing cobbles, just as his pen searches for holes in judgement. He has stared at the sun, wondering where its brightness has gone.

'Karl, poor eyesight is the burden of our office and our age,' the Director General had said. 'Our work is a *munus publicum*, old friend. We are entrusted with a duty vital for the safety of our people. You may leave the job, of course, when you find a replacement for yourself.'

Herr Weller remembers the lie on the Minister's lips. The way they smacked the words, as though the words themselves were bitter. He knows he will never leave this job. Not until he is fully blind. Perhaps not even then.

He knows, too, he could not survive on his salary from the library alone, and can barely complete the work he's given there. He cannot even shelve books anymore.

The other men at the library dislike him. They avoid him, as if old age and blindness were contagious. He has heard the Grimm brothers joke behind his back. Jacob called him a *stinkstiefel* – a smelly boot, a grouch.

How long ago had that been? How many words has he read since?

At the library and at home he is surrounded by the never-ending dreams of writers. They are legion. They write through days and nights, while he must stop to eat, to sleep. Each Monday, the manuscripts are brought to his front door, bundles of wood from an infinite forest. Hearing the paper flutter in his cramped room, he's imagined it still alive. As though it continues to grow. No matter how many words he cuts, this forest will not stop. Herr Weller knows the seeds, the thoughts behind the words, will never end.

*

Monday, there is a note on top of Herr Weller's books, the Director General's seal across the crease. They are sending an assistant to train. Someone to help with his work.

The next day the knock comes at his door. He bids them to enter. He feels the hands of his clock.

'You are two hours late.'

'I'm early. Your clock is wrong.'

He knew it was a woman before he heard her voice. The flowery soap. The murmur of layered cloth.

He puts his clock to his ear and hears nothing. He has lost time again. He has hardly felt its passage since losing so much light. As she steps past him, he wonders again if he will be immune to time when his sight is gone. Will time stop?

They work in silence. He gives her texts with smaller print then checks them. He cuts the text she leaves by half. She is quiet when she reads his re-edit. When her voice comes it carries something. *Sadness? Anger?* He cannot read her.

'Herr Weller, do you believe in this work?' she says, at last.

He tells her what he once said to a publisher: 'Would you send a daughter into the streets of Marburg naked? Language is the same. It must be cloaked or it is obscene. We are the dressers. Sometimes nothing but a pair of stockings is needed. When necessary, a full nun's habit.'

A week later, she asks him again, 'But do you *believe* in this work?'

This time he sorts through his papers until he finds one with the Minister's seal. He hands it to her. It is a letter he knows by heart:

> *Herr Weller,*
> *Censors are not responsible for the success of their venture. And even if they should be of the opinion that the dutiful exercise of their profession is pointless, or even counterproductive, oversights are inexcusable. While the actual success of actions against printed material remains uncertain, under all circumstances, nonetheless, the commandments of appointed authority exercise a healing power.*

He does not tell her this letter was a response to a letter of his. A letter he's wished, many times, he'd never sent. A letter he wrote when he was young and still had hope and, therefore, a sense of what was hopeless. A letter written when his sight was perfect, when he could clearly see the words *futile and impossible task* as he penned them.

She does not speak. She folds the letter and returns to her book, and he to his.

*

Herr Weller's right eye is stronger than his left, so he favors it. The magnifying glass swells it to something monstrous. A Cyclops that eats words.

He excises, now, for comfort: The black passages are easy on the eyes. He can read those without the glass's aid.

With her there, he works without pause. He cuts and slashes, as though the forest has become a jungle, his pen a machete. He risks a fine by working so carelessly, but he cannot stop himself.

He sets down his glass with a sigh, as if it were heavy as a shovel.

'I could read for you,' she says.

'I am not a child.'

'Your eyes must be tired. I was told I *should* read for you.'

'I am quite able to read for myself.'

Until weeks pass and he is not. His lamp now but a faint glow. The words black lines, as though the book had censored itself. He pretends to read for days until her voice is at his side.

'Herr Weller, your text is upside down.'

Then the pages are gone from his desk and she reads them aloud.

He stops her with a finger in the air.

'This is not music. If you must read, do so as if each word were a brick in a wall, no different than the one before or after. Do not *inflect* so.'

And she tries, with him stopping her, to tell her what to change, where to cut.

For a time she reads in this deadened pitch, her voice as flat as a frozen lake. But she cannot help herself. Her voice thaws.

It becomes a river through the mountains, moving down, leveling off in meadows, down valleys, rising in rapids, until he cannot help but be lost in her aria of words, until he forgets to stop her. To censor.

She says to him, 'Listen, Herr Weller, listen to this...'

*

Herr Weller does not hear the end of the story.

'I would not lose a word. Would you?' she says.

Herr Weller says nothing, for he is asleep. He dreams of forest fires. It is blindness's only gift; his dreams have become more vivid than ever. Soon, Herr Weller will see only with his eyes closed.

She nods as if they are in agreement, covers him with a heavy blanket, and spreads it to his chin.

She is at last free to inspect his room. There is a painting on the wall, an unimaginative landscape that barely stops her eye. She scans the bindings of his books, few in number and neatly stacked.

She startles at her reflection in the looking glass. She laughs. The mirror is covered with dust, as is everything here. She saw herself blurred, as if she were a ghost. How strange, she thinks, to have a mirror filled by a face that can never see it. Her hand moves to brush away the dust, then it stops.

Instead, she moves closer. Till the mirror contains

only her face. She bunches her hair atop her head. She smiles.

I look biblical, she thinks. *No. Not biblical…*

Herr Weller stirs at her giggles.

Like Scheherazade. Only my stories do not save me, but themselves.

In the dusty mirror, the candle's flicker snags her eye. A distant fire in a fog. Its flame carries a message she cannot read, but it shadows her thoughts and chills the room.

She drops her hair and her smile.

II

Jacob Grimm does not turn back until he reaches the first meadow. From here, the town below looks toy-like. He sees the spire of the church casting its long shadow over the square, like a knife above bread. From this distance, the few people in the streets of Marburg seem frozen in their morning routines.

Halfway up the mountain he remembers today's appointment at the library. He's already on the wrong side of the Director General. Missing today will surely push him further from the right side. Jacob's steps slow, as if the spectral hand of responsibility and office tug him back towards the town. He suddenly feels the steep incline, the chill in the air he underdressed for.

Then the sun tops the tree line ahead. An owl whoops

its last defense of darkness, and day slides in at Jacob's chest. He continues upward. He is nearly there.

*

The old woman waits by her fireplace. She does not turn as Jacob stoops to enter the tiny hut. The woman stirs the logs in the fire, ignoring Jacob and the sparks that swarm her hands.

She doesn't see his nose wrinkle at the dirt floors and air, thick with cooked fat and mildewed fruit. But she feels it. She knows the town folks' looks. Their soft hands. Their weak stomachs when it comes to butchering animals. She lost her son to the town.

Jacob busies himself, removing his ledger, uncorking his inkpot, smoothing the paper. Then he folds his hands and waits. He is learning to be patient. He is twenty eight, and it is not an easy lesson. But the old woman, who could be one hundred, is an excellent teacher. She moves by a clock that confounds him. Infinitely slower than the ticks and chimes of the town below.

The old woman totters around the room as if she is alone. There is grace in her crooked body, nimbleness in her hands as she slices *kartofi* into the pot. She mumbles something Jacob cannot hear, a recipe or a reminder to herself.

The trace of onion makes his stomach rumble. The old woman, as if she has just noticed him, tears a heel of bread and offers it. Her mouth is a wrinkle, as flat as the many others in her face. But her eyes smile. They flicker with fire.

The bread is still warm, but it is the smile and not the bread that makes Jacob grateful. Some days, the hike up the mountain is for nothing. Some days, she stuffs him with food but is stingy with words, her eyes anchored on the fire and whatever stories unfold in that stone proscenium.

'She's half mad,' he's told Wilhelm. 'Alone on the mountain, it's a wonder she still speaks at all.'

He's never told Wilhelm the whole truth: that he's a little afraid of her. It's not her ugliness or stony gaze. It's her silence. In it, Jacob feels as thin and transparent as a pane of glass. As if his tailored coat and silk scarf, the myriad books in his head, all total less than a single stone in her fireplace.

Today's silence is a lighter one, a cloud that will soon pass. The trip is not wasted. Today there will be stories.

*

The old woman has her pre-story rituals. Food prepared, the next day's firewood cut. Jacob carries the wood from yard to house. As he stacks it, he thinks how some wood becomes books, and some only fire and ash. Jacob wonders if paper has memories of being a tree. The old woman's place fills his head with strange thoughts.

Again, he thinks *perhaps she's a witch*, like the ones that live and die in her stories.

She wipes her hands on her apron and lights her pipe. Jacob tries not to fidget. He wonders if she's changed her mind. Perhaps she's not in the telling mood.

Then, abruptly, she sits across from him.

She begins as she always begins. 'Once, it happened...'

Jacob listens and writes. His memory is flawless, but the writing lends seriousness to their time. And there is the shading. A changed detail here, a better word there. His quill wrestles and subdues the old woman's tale.

She must see writing as magic, Jacob has thought.

He is not wrong. Because she cannot read, because she's seen real magic, she knows every book is a book of spells.

*

The old woman stops. She knows not to tell a story too fast. One must withhold. Suspend. At least in stories, if not in life, the ending can be delayed.

She refills Jacob's bowl despite his protests.

'I'm stuffed like a turkey.'

'You're as skinny as a wheat stalk,' she says. She always says.

Jacob sighs, hands on belly. He explains how he spends all his money on books, that the salary of a librarian couldn't fill a child's palm.

'You can't eat a book.'

'Not with your stomach,' he says, and she laughs and at last shows her teeth or what's left of them. It's a variation on banter they've had dozens of times. As if she is forgetful, or truly mad, or simply craves the repetition. Jacob does not know.

*

Jacob's quill halts moments after her words. Today's story was especially beautiful. He has heard it before, from others, but never spun with such tension.

Later, he believes he'll make it even better. More colorful details. A less ambiguous moral. A story of, and for, the German people. Like Wilhelm, Jacob believes he saves what must never be lost. He hopes, in some way, it restores the balance of what they cut as censors at the library. Creation and preservation to offset destruction.

*

Later, Jacob falls asleep. The mountain air, the stew, the drowsy heat of the fire, all this quilted the cover of sleep. His chest rises and falls with artless dreams. They are wishes thrown like doves in the sky. A thick book in everyone's hands. Everywhere.

The old woman considers waking him. But the sun sinks and descending the mountain after dark is not wise.

Instead, she covers him with a rough blanket. She

caps his ink and straightens his pages. She squints at the words and tries to see her story in them. If she could read, she'd see he's taken many liberties: sanded corners, shifted settings. If she could read, she'd approve all of them. She knows the teller builds the story his own way. So it's always been and must be.

She feels empty. It's always that way after a telling, as if one gives away something that cannot return. She turns to the fire. She watches flames lick stone and eat wood. In the hopping flames she sees a shadow. There are dark things in the night, she knows, and cities crowded with monsters more terrifying than those of her stories. They wait in a history that has not yet happened.

The fire is hot, but a chill travels through her old bones.

III

The chill crosses not just Marburg or Prussia, but all of Europe.

Heinrich Heine feels it at his desk in Paris. Here, where his voluntary exile became imposed, he grapples with a poem.

The poem before him is dead. In fact, it was never alive. Its words are rusted nails, its metaphors cheap decoration. Heine's attention has been turned out the window, toward the night and its chill. The indifferent fire of stars.

Heine flips the paper of his lifeless poem. He writes

what they've all seen. The fire and the shadow. The light and that which consumes it.

He stares east, towards home. Prussia, where they banned his work and fenced him with spies. He's found it good for the writing, useful to have things to push against. Yet tonight it does not help. His eyes again fix on a star that blazes in the sky.

Fire is a time machine. He plucks a memory from childhood. The people of Düsseldorf gathered around the Easter fire, celebrating the resurrection of Christ. Spring. He hears songs. Sees the glow of young men's faces.

He recognizes none.

As a poet, he understands this is not memory but vision.

In his vision, it is not wood but words that burn. The young men, strangers, chant and roar as sparks climb the night.

The very words before him, 'Where they burn books they will soon burn men.' These too will blaze in the flames.

· · ·

REFRACTED

Stephanie Wilderspin

PINK

I didn't realise I'd been chewing my tongue until Gabriella makes a sound of disgust. And, all at once, I am aware of the dull pain in my mouth. In sections, as if to mirror the patterns of my teeth.

There's a small crease between Gabriella's sharp, furrowed brows. They're recently plucked, starker than normal. 'Comes with being Mediterranean,' she told me once. 'You spend a fortune on razors.'

I look at the table, avoiding her sharp gaze.

'Sorry. I didn't know I was doing it.'

She tuts as she pulls the cinnamon roll towards herself and cuts into it with her knife. 'Abby, please don't gain another annoying habit.'

It's nice that you think I have control over my own body and mind. It feels like the only thing that's truly mine is the anxiety.

I didn't realise that bad habits followed me. I don't want my past here. Not with you.

I sigh. 'I'm sorry. I'll try.'

'Good. Stopping your leg-shaking is infuriating enough. But I can't stop your tongue.'

You can't get annoyed at me for something I didn't know I was doing.

You can stop my tongue if you kiss me.

'I'm sorry.' I look down at the table to where she has placed a carefully cut half of a cinnamon roll in front of me.

Gabriella shrugs. 'It's fine. Instead of chewing your tongue, I want you to chew on the best cinnamon rolls in Birmingham. I am your guide here, after all.' She gives me a soft smile; the kind that causes something to jump in my chest and replace any semblance of annoyance that had just been sat there. 'Buen provecho,' she says as she takes a bite, but all I can focus on is the sugar that clings to the saliva coating her lips.

YELLOW

I allow the silence to fill up Angela's small office even though it means my leg will start to shake. Three books shoved on the shelf above her computer. Five hooks on the back of the door. Chipped gold nail varnish on Angela's ring finger. Why that colour? It clashes with the concerned expression on her face. But matches the dull fluorescent light that flickers on the ceiling.

'Abigail,' she chooses a different note for each syllable of my name, 'how has this week been?'

I shrug. The papers on her desk don't quite align with the corner of the table. I adjust them so there is an equal gap on either side. I exhale. I catch Angela's gaze and give a small smile. 'Sorry.'

'It's fine. Have you been eating?'

> *I told my housemate, Harper, that the only food I could imagine eating was pasta with chopped up hotdogs. The next morning, I found a packet of frankfurters on the table.*

I nod.
'Enough?'

'Yeah. Three meals.'

'That's good, Abby. Good...' She scribbles something in her notepad.

What are you writing? What's in the file you're keeping on me? Who gets to see it while I'm not allowed to read the summary of my own downward spiral?

I can't make sense of it. All I want to know is if you have been able to.

'How is the new medication going? Better, now you're off the SSRIs?'

I think they're working. The same familiar emotions crop up, but they feel muffled now, as if they're wrapped in cotton wool. They're still there, pressing into my brain. Just not as hard as before, I guess. I have to wash my hands for twenty seconds now. I have three bottles of anti-bac in my bag.

'Yeah.'

'Have you spoken to your family recently?'

Mum keeps calling, but I keep it to texts. My sister Amy was going to visit this weekend,

*but Harper said I should cancel. She says that
Amy tends to make things a lot worse. I haven't
replied to Dad's texts in a year. If I tell them,
then I have to explain, and I don't have the
words for it yet.*

'Yeah, a bit. Just over the phone.'
'I thought they lived nearby?'

*They do. Same town, actually. But still distant
in the ways that matter.*

Angela looks at her watch. 'Abigail, these sessions are
designed to work around you.'

*No, they're designed to work around the leaf-
lets they keep giving me on 'low mood'. As if a
quickly made Word document could shut these
abhorrent thoughts up.*

'Okay.'
'And there's no point in these meetings unless you talk
to me about what's happening inside your head. We can
evaluate them together.'
'Okay.'
'Would it help if I made my questions more direct?'
'Maybe.'
She holds the pen up against the paper and pushes

her lips up into what she must think is a warming smile. I'm sure I'm not her easiest patient.

'Why did you try to kill yourself?'

As soon as I get home, I open up Rightmove, click on a city I've never been to. I arrange a viewing for the first flat I see.

Harper doesn't talk to me for a month afterwards.

RED

The nosebleeds start when I am seven. The tissue pressed against my nose struggles to hold any more liquid, so the blood starts to seep onto my hand. As I walk across the landing, I can hear Mum trying to say calming things through her own tears, but Amy isn't listening. Her small, five-year-old lungs have created a barrier of ringing screams so she's inaccessible. I'll see her cry like this again when she's ten, thirteen, twenty-two. This time, it's because she doesn't like the idea that she won't get to see Grandad again. After Mum told us, tears started to cascade down Amy's round cheeks. When the screams started and my parents darted to comfort her, I snuck up the stairs. As I pressed the door to the office shut, I felt a warm liquid trickle down to my lips. I instinctively licked it and tasted metal.

I press and hold the rewind button on the VCR and tap at the + button on the TV so the volume bar blinks up 'full'. Nestled in the worn padding of Dad's office chair, I rip off part of the toilet roll and scrunch it in my fist. I watch the tape through three times. If I do more than that, the tape will break, or Dad will yell again, or Amy will cry again tomorrow. She does cry the next day, even though I stop at three.

The nosebleeds will come back when I'm a teenager. I will hide the blood with my hand and ask to go to the toilet. People will knock on the cubicle door, but I will perch on the toilet seat until the bell rings for lunch. Sometimes, I will go and get my bag. Other times, I will walk home without it.

I'm twenty-five and I drip blood onto the white kitchen tiles within an hour of meeting Gabriella. She steps in front of me to clean them before I can even think. It makes me realise before I've even unpacked the boxes in my new room that this is her home. It will never be mine.

But for now, my seven-year-old self takes in the bright colours coming through the glass over the TV screen and tries to stop the nosebleed. I'll learn to handle them in time.

But the blood will never quite stop.

BLUE

'You never told me why you left Essex.'
Gabriella is curled up on the sofa like she often is,

hair splayed, ready to leave strands that I'll still find days later. Her head rests on the edge of my thigh. I absent-mindedly fidget with the splitting ends that fall into my lap.

I take a breath, buy myself time.

I was twenty-five and living in the town I'd always lived in. Felt like I hadn't lived at all, honestly.

Everyone looked at me funny after the incident. Like I could explode or fall apart at any moment. They weren't wrong.

I shrug. 'There are more companies here and more accounting jobs. Plus, I just wanted a change.'

She nods. I know she gets it. We've talked before about Alicante, how it felt like a trap for tourists but also for her. I feel like there's more to her motive for leaving. But I guess we have that in common.

We return to a comfortable silence, broken only by whatever shit we've let play on TV. But I can't focus. I never can when she's next to me. It's fucking annoying, honestly. Caring this much.

'We've only known each other for a few months. Why does it feel like I've known you for years?' Gabriella doesn't look at me, just at the TV.

*It's different living with you than with
Harper. When I moved here, we fell into
a rhythm immediately: eat together after we
get back from work, go to brunch on Sundays,
so you can show me your favourite places
in the city. Fall asleep watching TV.*

*Sometimes it feels like fate intervened.
Like how it was your house that came up first
on the search; that you were the one that opened
the door and not the other housemates; that our
rooms shared a wall.*

*The day I moved in, you answered the door
in your sports bra and shorts, and I knew I was
fucked. Then it got worse when I could earn eye
rolls from you with a simple bad joke, because it
meant I had your attention. I'd won the reluctant,
endeared smile that would play across your face.*

*Sometimes, I don't know if it's because we're too
different, or just dangerously too similar.*

When I don't answer, Gabriella gives a smile. 'I don't
know either. I'm just glad we ended up friends.'

*But I do know how it happened. You're in a
foreign country. I'm in a foreign city, but some-*

times it feels like I'm trapped in a brain
I have no control over. But there's a common
denominator: we're both being eaten away
at by our own loneliness. But to utter those
words would remind me how true they are,
and I don't want that right now. I want
to wait in this hope; the same one I want you
to have too. Just a little longer.

'I'm glad too. You make a good lasagne,' I say with a wink.

She gives me a light punch on the shoulder and hits play on the next episode.

PURPLE

It was not a tragedy because that
implies that there is an ending.
What I was intending to be the conclusion
became an interlude. I wanted a full stop
but the lines on my wrists were hyphens
the holes from the stitches were colons.

ORANGE

She's two hours late for dinner and she's mad at me?
Why is she mad, she's not allowed to be mad when
she's done this and not thought about me; she's so——

'Abby, stop.'
'I can't,' I say.

*—and I say that bit out loud because it's true
and the thoughts will get worse if I stop I need
to be busy I need her to eat and be well but
my brain hurts and why did I just slam the
cupboard fuck I could see her jump why am
I doing this to her I care about her so much it
overwhelms me but my brain is saying horrible
things such horrible horrible things and I can't
tell where they start and I end*

'You're scaring me.'

*she's not allowed to be scared she can't hear these
thoughts I have and I want to keep her safe from
that and if I stop I'm scared what will happen I
care about her so much I want her to be okay I've
only ever wanted her to be okay but she doesn't
listen she never listens she isn't listening now*

'Abby, I'm fucking fed up of this shit.' I stop.
'What the fuck do you mean?'
'I've thought it for a while, but this is too much.
She sighs. 'You scare me. You terrify me, honestly.'

And I let out a laugh. One of disbelief.

But I can't explain to her that she's getting the watered-down version of what I could be and what I have been. She's not allowed to be scared when she's not the one stuck with this bullshit. This always happens and it's happened again and what's the point what's the point what's the point I'm stuck and—

Does she fucking know I'm ill? Does she really know? It was Harper in A & E with me when I tried to off myself she doesn't get to hear these thoughts she gets to see the new me the Birmingham me the one that gets to casually mention I have depression not the Essex version where everyone knows I had a fucking meltdown

'You only think of yourself.'

Bullshit

The problem is that I only ever think of you. When things get bad, I think, at least Gabriella and I will eat dinner together and watch Netflix, or I text you and hope to get heart emojis back. The worst times are when I picture a future together that I know we'll never have. Where I finally kiss you when you

give me that reluctant, endeared smile. That
I get to run my hands up the sides of your rib
cage, get to show you just how much I think
about you.

I know I'd fall in love with you. But only if
you'd let me.

But I only bring sadness. I don't want that
for you.

As usual, I say nothing.

And she says, 'I think you should move out.'

It's her turn to slam the door now.

BLACK

'I'm still mad at you,' Harper says as she looks to the sea. But her tone is ruined as she scrunches her nose, as if that's what anger looks like. 'You can come back home and beg as much as you want, but I'm picturing all the ways to torture you right now.'

'I know.' A smile sneaks onto my lips. 'I'm sorry.'

'You're a terrible person and I hate you.'

'No, you don't.'

She presses her lips together, but a laugh comes out in a splutter.

'Fuck!' she shouts. A nearby mother tuts. Harper

sticks her middle finger up at her.

'You're right, I don't, and that makes me madder. But also…' She looks at me, face softer than before. Not pity. Never pity, and I'm thankful for that. 'I'm glad you're okay. And also, I'm going to smack that bitch one for hurting you like that.'

A warmth falls across me, and only part of it is due to the sun.

'I appreciate it, but she was right.'

'Don't care if she has a PhD in why you're a prick. We all know that. But she didn't give you a chance, and that's her loss. But means I get you back. Even though you *abandoned* me and I had to move into my parents' house.'

'I could never really leave you, Harper. You know that.'

'I get why you left, Abby. Honestly, as much as I'm fucking mad at you for forcing me to pay two months' rent all on my own, I think you needed it. After you—' Her words falter, and she gestures at the lines on my wrist, not covered like they normally are. Not in this heat. She kicks at me with her flip-flop, our legs dangling over the promenade. 'She doesn't deserve you if she's not willing to learn how to handle you. You feel things so deeply.'

'Ha, yeah. Tell me about it.'

'You're worth learning about, Abby.'

I watch the waves ride up the beach, and slink back to the murky water that spreads to the horizon. Every time they hit the sand, I tap my finger against my thumb. I count how long it takes for the message to make its journey. Six seconds. Tap. Six seconds. Tap. Six seco—

Harper leans her head on my shoulder. Water blurs my vision of the sea. I can still hear the waves, though.

Six seconds tap. Six seconds tap. Six seconds tap.

'I'm so sorry, Harper.' Tap.

'Don't be sorry, dickhead.'

Tap. Tap. Tap.

'It's not fair.'

Tears fall onto my hands. I hit a drop as I tap.

'Yeah, it's not fair on *you*.' She rests her open palm on the concrete between us. Tap. 'That's not how this works.'

'Isn't it?'

I feel her shake her head against my shoulder. 'Of course it isn't, you prick.' Tap. 'Bad things happen.'

'I did so many bad things, Harper. To you, to everyone.' The sobs I've been holding in for an hour, fuck, been holding in since the Incident, fall out of me and won't stop.

I press my finger into my thumb. Harder every six seconds.

'That was just one part of Abigail that did that then. But there are other parts to you too. One part that likes to listen to the same album on repeat until you ruin it for everyone. Another part leaves the empty milk carton in the fridge.'

I give up timing the taps. I just dig my nails into the palm of my hand.

'But I also love the Abigail that checks the oven is off three times or has screaming panic attacks because she dropped a damn jam jar.'

I rest my hand over her palm. Squeeze.

'All those make up a whole Abby. That we love despite your regular breakdowns. So stop apologising for things outside of your control.'

She clamps her fingers round my hand. 'You wanker.'

I can try and sort all my thoughts and emotions and experiences, and count them like I do the steps I take or the amount of times I flick the light switch before I can get into bed. But in the end, all colours mix to black.

· · ·

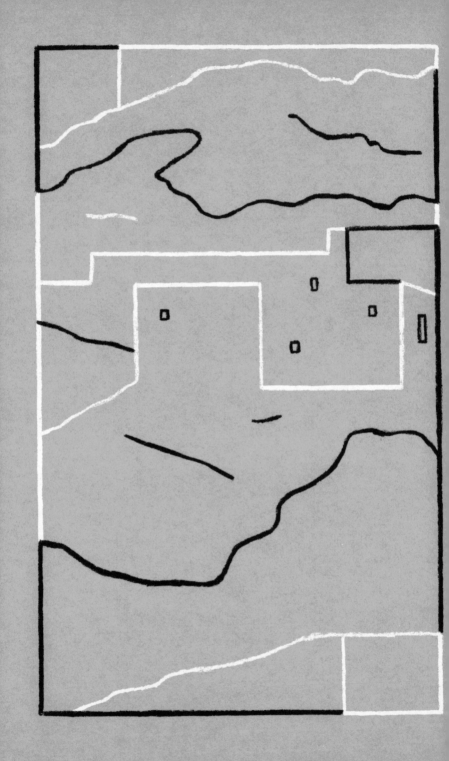

FORTRESS

Catherine Rudolph

---

n the kitchen her dad, in his favourite apron, was cutting the fillet. The meat, held in place by a carving fork, was opened with a stainless-steel blade, sunk in and drawn back and forth like a violin bow. Her father, the concert violinist, had watery red smears across his front, where he'd wiped his hands. The apron had a dancing crayfish – also wearing an apron – on the front. Claws held above its head, whiskers out at odd angles, the crayfish had what she perceived to be a joyous gleam in its small black eyes.

She had never seen a crayfish, not in real life. They were from a time before hers, when the Empire extended all the way to either coast and far up to the North. A time when you could go to the beach and swim in the ocean all day, leaving only when the wind would pick up and blow cold across the water. Her parents spoke about it, but not as often as they used to. They went diving every weekend for crayfish in those days. Her dad described it to her and her brother as a forest, underwater: a mass of slippery brown tubes, congealing in knots and splitting out into fluttering tendrils, trunks swaying in the water like strands of hair rising up from the ocean floor. He told them about the way crayfish swim, with their tails propelling them backwards through the water, so when you reached for one they shot away from you, but still faced you in their retreat, as if to say: 'Better luck next time!'

They sat down to eat at eight o'clock, after the evening news. There was much talk of what was happening outside: more uprisings on the farms, buildings being burned, houses looted and one family of four found dead in their living room. The littlest boy had already been dressed in his pyjamas for the night.

She remained silent for the conversation and got up only to clear the table. The plates had the remains of vegetables and pieces of fat, now congealed, which she scraped into the bin. She stacked the dishes neatly then stood looking at the thin soap-line left on the sides of the sink. She was startled to feel arms wrap around her from behind. Her mother leaned in to place a cheek against hers.

'We'll never let anything happen to you,' her mother said, turning her round to look in her eyes. 'You're in the safest place you could be.' She kissed her forehead.

She stayed there by the sink and thought of the kind of people who could cut a boy's stomach open. It was not a cold act, not removed like the things they learnt about in history class. She thought about the things happening more and more on the farms. 'A revolt of unprecedented violence', the news reporter said.

For a while, she had wanted to be a crayfish, until her brother told her that you kill them by steaming while they're alive. Her parents placed them, still flapping, in a big steel pot and secured the lid. Every now and again, the pot would clang on the stove as the crayfish flapped their tails against the sides. Even with the lid fastened tight, her brother said, you could hear a high-pitched whistling. It was the sound of the crayfish screaming as they were being boiled alive.

The fortress was white. It sat upon a hill at the edge of a forest. At the highest point you could see the mass of dirty houses below, like a carpet of insects glittering in the sun. Inside, the streets were uniformly pristine. The walls were made of pale stone or, for the more luxurious, marble. The fortress was surrounded by a wall of the same pale stone, three metres high and topped with electric fencing.

People came from outside to clean the houses. They entered the gates every day, presenting identification cards with both of their names. Inside, the people were called Mary and John, but outside, they had names she'd never heard of.

Her family had Mercy. Mercy looked after her and her brother when her mother went back to work. She took them to the park every day and pushed them on the swings. She made

Maltabella every morning before walking them to school and on Saturdays, after the park, Mercy played the memory game with them, sitting on the scratchy carpet in the patch of sun.

Her earliest memory was of Mercy: Mercy sitting on the boards of the merry-go-round up the hill. The merry-go-round was red, bright in the dry grass. Mercy faced her, her legs stretched out on the ground. She remembered something being wrong – she was crying, willing Mercy to come down the hill and hold her.

One spring, nearing her thirteenth birthday, Mercy disappeared for a while. When she asked her mother about it, her mother said that Mercy was taking a little holiday. Mercy came back not looking at all like she had been on holiday. She struggled under a load of washing, her lips were cracked and there was a dullness in her eyes that hadn't been there before.

At night, she overheard her parents talking about it.

'Do you think it's infectious?' Her mother sounded distressed.

'They're not sure. Either way, she can't keep coming here. People will notice.'

She heard chair legs scrape the floor as her father got up from the table.

'We have to help her.'

'I'm not putting this family at risk, even for Mercy.'

'Mercy is family,' her mother said.

When they told her Mercy had died she didn't say anything. She remembered the time she'd spilled spaghetti bolognese on the couch when she was watching TV, which she shouldn't *have been doing while eating. Mercy scolded her, but she spent the next two hours scrubbing away at the fabric so her mother wouldn't see. Mercy always said white was the worst to get clean.*

Her mother came home from the mall one day soon after Mercy's death and announced that they were having a new couch delivered. They had two couches already, and not much space left in the house, though it was a fairly big one – but not as big as the others further up the hill, her mother would say. The couch came and three silent men brought it in on their shoulders. It was large and white. Her mother spent the next two hours moving furniture, or getting the men to move it, but couldn't decide on the right space for the couch. Eventually, the men had to return home and the couch was left standing in the middle of the room.

*

Their writing workshop was in the Herzhog B room.

'It feels a bit "guilty white girl", you know? Like, you're the outsider looking in, like you have special access to an empathy they don't,' Clara said. She nodded, the words cutting only a little.

'Ya, I was worried about that.'

'The suburbia feeling was nice though,' Helen added and she gave her a small smile. There was a pause as everyone stared at their laptop screens. Her legs were restless under the table.

Dominic cleared his throat.

'I think we need to move on from this same old story,' he said. He was good-looking, in a heavy-set way, and wore a leather jacket, even in summer. 'Honestly it's been thirty years, it doesn't matter what colour you are.'

Her forehead creased. 'Uhhh, yes it does. How can you drive through Camps Bay or anywhere – Newlands, Rondebosch, Khayelitsha –' she gestured vaguely, 'and still think that?'

'But the Black people in your story were, like, pretty one-dimensional?' Clara looked at her enquiringly. 'At least, they didn't seem to have any agency.'

'Wouldn't it be helpful,' Helen ventured, 'if you had the point of view of a Black character? So we can see what it's like from the other perspective.' Helen's voice was like child medicine. It really pissed her off sometimes.

'I can't write a POC character. I don't know what that experience is like.'

'But you can imagine; you can be empathetic,' Clara said.

She took a deep breath. 'Don't you think, instead of imagining people's stories and telling them for them, we should just give people the opportunity to tell their own stories?'

'But then, what's the point of being a writer?' Clara countered. 'Like, can I only write about what it's like to be a white, English-speaking South African? Or about motherhood? I have experiences beyond that. *Human* experiences.'

'I just can't tell stories that aren't mine. I can't.'

Dominic unfolded his arms and opened his mouth again, but then leant back and looked at the ceiling.

Later, she received an email from him:

> *Dear Cat,*
> *I meant no offence in the meeting today. I think it's all a matter of sensitivity; Annie Proulx wrote* Brokeback Mountain, *and she's a woman, but she did a lot of research. I know it's a difficult subject, but I think the writer's main concern should be Truth. I found there was truth in that story.*

There was a link to an article with Proulx speaking about her reflections on life 'in the West'. The email ended with: 'Anyway, we should go for coffee and talk about this further. You're an interesting person.'

She rolled her eyes and got up. Dominic was the last person she would go for coffee with. In the bathroom mirror she inspected her gums; the dentist had given her a special soft-bristled brush to stop her from damaging them. Pulling her lips back, she bared her teeth at herself, feigning, for a second, the face of an angry dog. Then she smiled, as she would with a child. When brushing she made a conscious effort to be gentle. She rinsed and spat. 'Truth' was bullshit.

She couldn't pinpoint exactly when she had changed *Meisie* to Mercy in her head. She didn't want to believe that that was what she had called her. What her mother, who really had cried, who really had cared, had called her.

Meisie: girl.

She remembered visiting Meisie, somewhere far out where there were no trees. The corridors were filled with people, some with their backs against the wall, legs stretched before them, others lying on the floor. The rooms were full of beds that looked like old sanatorium beds from movies. There were no curtains dividing them, just rows of beds, like a dormitory.

She tried not to look left or right as they walked along the row to Meisie's bed. Meisie was thinner than she had ever seen a person, her skin dry, like there was a layer of ash covering it. Meisie's sister, Cynthia, spoke in Xhosa and gestured to her and her mother. Meisie didn't move.

'Look, Nana, look who has come to visit you,' Cynthia said, motioning her forward.

She peered into Meisie's face. Meisie tried to sit up, a smile cracking her lips. There were sores on her mouth and an intensity in her unblinking eyes.

'Hello Meisie,' she said, and her voice broke. Meisie reached out and touched her hand, and she held Meisie's hand, crying.

Her mother wiped her eyes and leaned in.

'How are you feeling?' She put her hand on Meisie's arm. Meisie nodded.

'Are the nurses taking proper care of you?'

Meisie nodded. They sat back and listened to Cynthia talk as she fed Meisie tiny spoonfuls of pink yoghurt, encouraging her to swallow. When her mother discussed the doctor's report, she stared out the window at the sky and the face-brick of surrounding buildings, wishing they could leave.

• • •

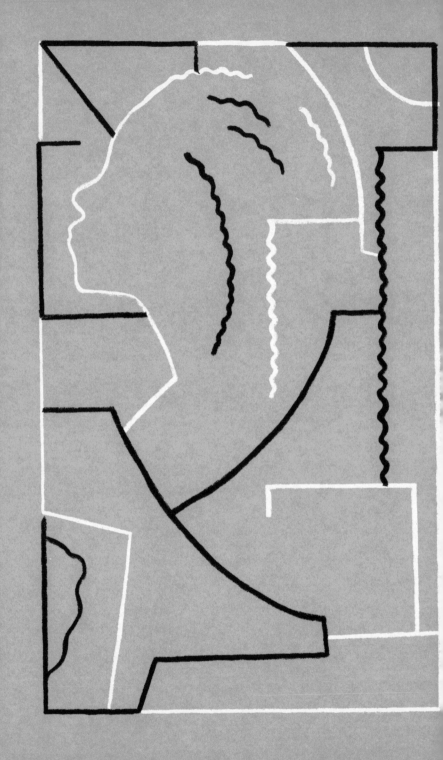

REFLECTIONS

Mubanga Kalimamukwento

M ummy was fanning herself on the sofa, yelling at the Africa Magic channel while I rummaged through her musty closet. I could've been nestled in the avocado tree, twisting a wheel for my latest wire car. But Mummy had this habit of sending me on useless errands, like fetching her dowdy yellow sweater even though it was the middle of August and melting hot. I scanned the tight space once more and groaned, 'I can't find it.'

The TV volume slid down, sofa springs creaked, and Mummy snapped back at me in her native tongue-threats, '*Iwe*, Twaambo, if I come in there and find it myself, *wapya!*' The *'you'll see'* jolted me up, straight into one of Daddy's trouser legs suspended on a plastic hanger. I tugged on them, soaked in Daddy's essence – Brut aftershave and Stuyvesant cigarettes – as the soft fabric fell and pooled around my skinned ankles. A belt was still hooked to one of the trouser loops. I lifted it, wrapped it around my waist twice, and smiled.

'Twaambo?'

I rolled my eyes and tried to unlatch the belt. 'I'm coming.' But it wouldn't budge. 'Has the thing locked itself again?' Mummy asked.

I tumbled out of the wardrobe onto the polished bedroom floor and fought with the buckle again, but the clip above my navel refused to move. I imagined what Mummy might say: *'You couldn't find what I sent you for, and yet there you are, standing in your father's trousers, eh?'* and my mouth went dry. 'Yes?' I whined back.

Mummy nudged the door again. *Click.* 'Well.' *Click.* 'Girl.' *Click.* 'Open.' *Click.* 'It!' Each snap of the door latch cut the air from my throat, pressing the brick walls into me while everything else stayed still. Leather belt, Mukwa wooden door, me – fixated on the word *girl.* Mummy flung it into every conversation as if merely saying would make it true.

'Don't call me that!' I spat, smacking my mouth too late. *'Chani?' 'What?'*

I darted my gaze around the room, each item my eyes landed on morphing into a weapon: shoes piled high on the rack, belts hanging from a bent nail in the wall, all waiting for Mummy to grab and flog me.

Mummy sucked her teeth. 'Use the scissors on the dresser to open it. NOW.'

I pictured her ripping through her *chitenge* wrapper to kick the door in and drag me out; my stomach clenched and I inched away. Instead, she said, 'Girl,' in a whisper-shout: 'Open this door!'

'No.'

A long moment passed, stuffing the room with a heavy silence until Mummy said, 'If you'll stay in there forever, then it's fine,' and stormed off. Each flap of her flip-flops on the corridor floor pushed the walls back into place, my ears popped, and sounds streamed in through the open window above my parents' bed: a sprinkler hissing into the grass, dogs barking in the distance, and the fluttering of avocado leaves. I turned and faced the mirror where a dusty-faced girl blinked back. Mummy often said that staring at my reflection too long would make me cross-eyed. The girl in the mirror snorted abruptly, then yanked the two silver studs out of her earlobes. She winced, ripped off her lacy green blouse and pulled out the polka dot bow crowning the kinky puff piled on top of her head. Panting, she shook her coils loose, grabbed the scissors, and slashed her hair until a boy emerged, eyes wet, cropped hair, white vest, oversized trousers knotted around a narrow waist, grinning: me. Just then, a car revved at the gate. As the rusty metal squeaked open, my stomach clenched a little. Past the singing crickets in the flowering hibiscus hedge, a yellow Accord hobbled over the rubble and parked outside the bedroom window. The driver's door swung open.

I squealed. 'Daddy!'

'*Mwanangu,*' he answered. '*My child.*'

I wobbled towards the door.

'Let me in, please?' Daddy asked, a few moments later. 'It's stuck.'

He coughed. 'Will you step back, then?'

I did, beaming as the door swung in after one thud. The bulb in the corridor cloaked him in a white glow as he crouched in, all rumpled clothes, wrinkled face and a smile twinning mine. He knelt for me to wrap my arms around his neck and kiss him on the cheek. His stubble tasted like black pepper and sweat.

'This daughter of yours,' Mummy exploded into the corridor from the kitchen. 'She's been locked in there all afternoon doing God knows what!'

Daddy peeled away from me, placed one hand on his chest and sighed. 'Did you try opening it?'

That's when Mummy saw me and screamed. 'What have you done to your hair?!'

I cowered behind Daddy.

'Wicked child!' Mummy screeched. 'Wicked, wicked child.'

Daddy frowned. 'But it's just hair. Won't it grow back?'

Mummy flitted past us, ignoring the synthetic wig

slipping from her head as she bent to gather my hair from the floor into balls. 'Just hair, eh! Like her tree-climbing is just a habit?' She spun back and narrowed her eyes at me. 'Now listen to me, girl.' She pulled down on her earlobe, as she'd have done to mine if Daddy wasn't there. 'If you don't stop with all this nonsense, one day those boys you call friends will stick something between those legs! And...'

My eyes widened. *And?*

But Daddy cut her off with a slap of his yellowed hand across her face.

I flinched, reliving the moment he'd slapped me for placing fourth instead of first in the last term of grade two. My palms moistened: I backed into the wall and whimpered.

Mummy and Daddy had fought before, shot hot, ugly words behind the veil of their bedroom wall, but this was the first time I'd seen any part of their bodies touch.

The creases on Daddy's forehead smoothened. 'None of that, *mwanangu,*' he soothed, bumping past Mummy to take my hand.

With my hair still in her hands, Mummy slumped into the bed and our eyes locked in the mirror, hers glistening with tears, and I wished I could attach my hair back if it would only bring back her voice. But then, she blinked, scrunched the ball of fuzz between her fingers and tossed it into the bin at the foot of their bed.

In the weeks that followed, Mummy clutched her

silence as tightly as a purse filled with money until my hair grew just long enough for her to say, 'Come here, *nkuluke*.' I planted myself on a cushion between her legs and closed my eyes while she twisted three-stranded *fikuti* into my hair. Mummy had called my hair a crowning glory; she'd stretched it with a white-hot metal comb straight off the brazier, tucked it into long synthetic braids, and lathered the roots with Blue Magic grease, but never before had she used it as a weapon. So, I bit my lip as she pulled my edges and waited for the next morning. While Mummy washed our laundry under the outside tap, I sneaked out of the yard and ran to the tin-metal barbershop near Woodlands Shopping Complex, where Daddy had his hair cut every other weekend.

'I'm shaving it off,' I announced to the barber, who was sweeping hair into a pile in the corner.

He stopped, 'What?'

'Like that,' I replied, pointing at a poster of a bald-headed man.

'But you have such lovely hair,' he protested.

I patted the tiny braids, the way Mummy would when I aired my school shoes outside or took the plates into the kitchen after dinner. 'The time is 8.10 on QFM,' announced a dusty black radio in the corner. I wavered, catching my reflection in the barber's mirror. If I ran back home right then, Mummy wouldn't even know I'd left. It would be as if I'd just crawled up the avocado tree again to bend bits of wire into toys. But I knew she'd find me, and say something like, '*Why can't you just make mud dolls like other girls?*'

No, I decided, plopping myself in the barber's chair. 'Make it as smooth as this,' I said, showing him my arm.

'Money first,' he said, stretching out his palm.

Finally, I could put the loose change Mummy let me keep after buying tomatoes to use.

'Yes.' I handed him five crumpled two-kwacha notes and swathed myself in one of his threadbare towels hanging on the chair.

'You'd look just like your father's son if not for that skirt,' the barber said to me when he was done. I ran my hand over my head and smiled as my skin prickled with goosebumps. *My father's son.*

I skipped back home, outrunning the children that sniggered 'girl-boy' at me, as I slipped between the straight line of houses leading to mine, and slinked into our yard through the itchy shrubs. Clean clothes were swinging on the line, and Mummy was humming in the kitchen. I lingered on the verandah until the aroma of her paprika chicken stew drew me slowly in.

'*Mwelesa!' Dear God!*' she cried, dropping her cooking stick. She snatched it back up and lashed me with it until she was breathless. 'What did I do to deserve such an insolent child?'

*

That's the Mummy I remember now as I scowl at the bathroom mirror, binding my breasts with a pair of worn tights, choking back tears as I wrap a *chitenge* around my pants. I squeeze myself into the white T-shirt with Daddy's face across the front and squint at the words etched across:

SCOTCH MAINZA
12/07/63–17/09/11
Always in our hearts

I'm glaring at the string of foul letters and numbers when someone knocks on the door.

'What?'

'*Mwanangu*, we have to go now,' Mummy says.

I stiffen and ball my fingers into a fist, ready to unravel them and scratch the word from her tongue. *Mwanangu. How dare she say it now? Taint Daddy's voice with her shrill one.* I spin around, unlock the door and glare at her. But the Mummy who looks in, eyes brimmed red, head covered in a black *chitambala*, is not the one who had forced me into this costume. 'Don't call me that.' It was supposed to be a scream, but it came out wobbly, like my legs. I grip the doorframe.

'If you don't come now, the cars will leave,' Mummy murmurs.

I kick a chipped floor tile and trail her into the sitting room. If I shut my eyes, I can pretend Daddy is still on the sofa, tapping his cigarette butt into an ashtray and swearing at the news. I can almost unsee the line of mattresses lying side by side on the carpet instead of four corduroy couches as I wade outside. Last night's fire is dying underneath an army-green tent pitched above the patch of grass where Daddy taught me how to ride my bike when I was five. I step into Elm Road, lined with cars on both sides, and inch my way to the one assigned to Mummy and me.

I slump in beside her and stare at the back of the driver's headrest while the car purrs on.

We roll onto Woodlands' pothole-riddled streets dotted with memories of Daddy. Through my tinted window, the memories reel past with the tree trunks: me, aged ten, waiting for Daddy outside G Club at our street corner where he gave me my first swig of Mosi beer; past the barbershop where we'd been shaving our heads every second Saturday of the month since I was eight; stopping at St Andrew's Church where Daddy brought me once aged twelve, after Mummy left for her parents village and swore on her dead mother's grave to never return.

Now Daddy's been reduced to a two-paged tribute being handed out by Aunt Hazel at the steps of the church. She trots to meet us. 'Here,' she says breathlessly, shoving a *chitenge* into me. I glance down and see Daddy's pants clinging to my thighs.

My chest tightens as I examine Mummy's face and

prepare my defence. The neat lines of frangipani trees fencing the church off from the road suddenly feel too close. I wipe my slick palms on my trousers. My *chitenge* must have slipped off as I was getting out of the car. But then Mummy croaks, 'Please, leave her,' and my mouth drops.

'I understand, *Mulamu*,' Daddy's sister whispers, darting her eyes everywhere but mine. 'We're all grieving, but this is a house of God. She can't go in dressed like… like that.' Aunt Hazel whispers the last word even though the other mourners are already staring.

Mummy straightens her shoulders. 'Or what?'

Aunt Hazel folds her arms and narrows her eyes.

'He didn't care then about her dressing, and he won't care now,' Mummy continues. She pulls me, and together we lumber into the massive, stained-glass-windowed building. The benches are crammed with people clicking their phones, but even the light tapping dies as Mummy and I walk past leaving only the screeching microphone at the podium waiting for the Reverend to speak. I tune him out when he does and focus on the photo of Daddy, which only four days ago hung on the sitting room wall but is now pitched on top of his coffin. I memorise the lines on his forehead, the *v* where his eyebrows meet, the crows' feet fanning out of the corners of his eyes, and his wonky smile over and over so that I'll remember him as he was in that picture: perfect. When the service is over, six grim pallbearers roll the coffin to the church door followed by pew after pew of mourners rising to peer into it, wail, dab their eyes and then snap out into the sunshine as if they didn't just see Daddy for the last time. Eventually, Mummy and I follow.

Daddy's supposed to be tucked between the silk sheets of a gleaming white box.

But the thing there, tiny cancer-eaten grey face sleeping behind the glass, isn't him. 'That's not my father,' I mumble.

'Be strong,' Mummy says, rubbing my back.

I shake her off. 'Look!' His nose is pinched, black lips burnt pink, and body collapsed into itself so that everything is too large on him, white shirt, striped tie, and hands placed above his chest. 'That – that is not my father,' I stammer in between short breaths.

Mummy leans into me. I jerk back, catching a whiff of nicotine, but it's only one of Daddy's scarves draped loosely around her neck. 'I know, *mwanangu*,' Mummy mutters, dissolving finally into sobs.

• • •

AIDEN SHAW'S PENIS

Ali Said

When they get it wrong, they get it spectacularly wrong. The Censors. Like now, this magazine; Aiden Shaw's penis. Ali's throat tightens. He cannot understand how they could have missed it. It is pretty sizeable. More than sizeable, really. It is quite something. His hands are shaking as he stands by the rack in the supermarket. They shake more while he hands over money at the till. Ali steps into the heat of the desert sun, looks over his shoulder, then sprints for home.

*

In the United Arab Emirates The Censors were an everyday part of Ali's life, like hearing the call to prayer or finding sand in his shoe. His earliest memory of them was a history book his aunt gave him when he was seven. It told stories of great leaders of the past: George Washington, Genghis Khan, Napoleon; their splendour revealed in simple prose and delicately drawn cartoons. His favourite, even then, was Catherine the Great. That small, round woman in a tiara who ruled an empire. Even then.

Catherine with her jewels, her cleavage, was not what angered The Censors. When Ali turned to the pages on Prophet Muhammad, they were scrawled over with a gold marker pen. It was not that the authors had inadvertently slandered him; no, it was the pictures. Images of the Prophet were forbidden. So gold stood between Ali and knowing what the holy man might have looked like. Only the occasional flash of robe or heel of sandal peeked out at the edges. Ali didn't mind; he loved the sparkling colour anyway. Gold was quite an unusual choice, black being the most common. It seemed to him different Censors chose different tools for their craft. He imagined them all seated at long tables, a psychedelic pot of pens in the middle like at kindergarten. Each one given an offending magazine or newspaper to colour in.

At nine Ali became obsessed with records. What

was biggest, tallest or fattest suddenly seemed very important. For his birthday, *The Guinness Book of World Records*. When he got to the section on the richest person it was covered in Tipp-Ex. Thick, lumpy, white Tipp-Ex across his lovely new book. He picked at it with his nail but made little progress. Later, he told his older cousin, Salman, about this. Salman had laughed, 'Tipp-Ex is the easy one! Just hold it up to the light and look at the back. You can see everything. Black pen is much worse.' At home Ali pressed the page to the bulb of his bedside lamp. Sheikh Zayed, President of the UAE, World's Richest Man. His wealth too great for his subjects to cope with.

News sometimes suffered the same fate. Ali's father bought the *Sunday Times* every Monday, it taking an extra day to reach Dubai. He would harrumph at an article, or maybe a whole page, that had been removed. Back then there was no way to discover what it was they were missing, or why. An absence only momentarily felt.

*

Ali sits on his bed with the magazine. Sky Magazine *had started to be sold in the Emirates in the early nineties. It is part of his transition to adulthood, he's certain. Until then his pop music addiction had been fed through* Smash Hits *in all its bright colours and shouty text. But* Sky *is different.* Sky *is grown up. It has a problem page, almost always about sex.*

It sometimes has topless women, their breasts always blacked out by The Censors. This issue has an interview with Tony Blair, who, Ali's grandad says, is going to make Britain a better place. But Ali's fingers skip over Tony. He turns to the centrefold, and there it is again. Under the heading The Freaks, *is a row of people in outlandish clothes. Some have gothic makeup, others carry implements he doesn't recognise. 'Britain is changing', he reads, but he can't focus on the words. Standing in the middle of the group is a man he's never seen before. Aiden Shaw. A porn actor, apparently. He stares at the camera, half a smirk on his face. He is naked, his thick penis hanging between his legs like a prize. Ali touches the page.*

*

Censorship was easy, in the eighties. Tape was so simple to cut and stick back together. Cassettes and videos would jump across offending words or scenes. So many times had Ali seen men and women on screen make their way to a bedroom then – in the flash of a Censor's scissors – awake in the next scene, fully clothed. On American soap operas people with big hair and shoulder pads would lean in for a kiss only to pull apart immediately. You had to feel for The Censors, his Islamic Studies teacher once said, the awful things they had to see in order to protect us. They couldn't look away from sin; they had to stare it right in the kissing mouth so the rest of us could live pure lives.

Every summer the family would flee the heat to his maternal grandparents' house in London. They would buy videos to take home, Dubai's one English-speaking TV channel providing too meagre an entertainment. On arrival their videocassettes would be confiscated. The Censors then watched them in a dark room somewhere, and you would get them back in two weeks. If you got them back. This went too for the endless home movies Ali's father took on his giant 'portable' video camera. Unfortunately, those always came back.

Sometimes, the unknown absences caused surprises. The first thing Ali could clearly remember spending his pocket money on was a Samantha Fox cassette. The first of many. Samantha's synthetic pop became wildly popular in the UAE, despite songs called things like 'Naughty Girls Need Love Too'. Ali became obsessed. He would flick frenetically through rows of counterfeit tapes looking for more Samantha. Always, more Samantha. But here her image was clean, her purity kept intact. For Ali, she was just a hardworking girl with a beautiful voice. The first summer back in London after embracing Samanthaholism, his uncle had roared with laughter. 'No wonder he's obsessed, what with those tits!' Ali had had no idea she was a topless model. Page 3. Everyone had seen them. How could she? How could they hide this from him?

But there was something else. Over time, Ali realised

the tapes he bought were all by feisty, take-no-shit ladies. Samantha, Kim Wilde, Belinda Carlisle. He didn't want to see their tits, he wanted to be them. At ten he had a poster of Belinda in a black dress, standing against a white brick wall wearing shocking-pink lipstick. And it was shocking. Ali told his sister that he wanted that shade of lipstick one day. She said boys didn't wear lipstick.

As the eighties slipped into the nineties Ali increasingly knew that it was not an absence he now felt but a presence. One he could not explain and he could not reveal. It kept growing. Aged twelve, his family holidayed in southern France. A handsome man with bronze skin and jet-black hair gave him windsurfing lessons. The summer after, on the long tube journey from Heathrow, a man in a tank top with bulging biceps sat next to him. Thirty years later, Ali would be able to visualise both of them completely. Their clothes, their lips, those biceps. It was as if he had cut their pictures out of the *Sunday Times* and kept them for his eyes only. Perhaps that's what every Censor did.

Ali had been a curious child, always wanting to learn. He read articles about the Iran–Iraq war, or how many hospital beds there were per person in the USSR, while his cousins were reading comics. But here he was on his own. Even as teenagers, no teacher was allowed to talk to them about sex, let alone deviant desire. No books in the library to help, no articles about Pride in the papers.

At fourteen, Ali fell in love with Michael. And with

Daniel a little bit, but mostly Michael. He would watch him across the classroom and know that he needed to be with him. It was a knowing that came before a realisation. Long before. The man on the beach, the biceps on the tube, they didn't make him something. Loving Michael didn't make him something. Did it? It was too hard to know when even the word was unspeakable.

Later that year Ali's mother returned from a trip to England with a book in her bag. *The Liar* by Stephen Fry. She did not seem to have enjoyed it much and it was tossed on the bookshelf. Bored one weekend, he picked it up. Soon his head was spinning. It would never have made it past The Censors. The book was a comedy; at least he thought it was. The story jumped around a lot, the narrator was untrustworthy, and entire chapters turned out to be false. But in it were the first descriptions of gay sex he had ever read. Ali frowned over a line about *the beast with two backs, or in this case, one back and a funny-shaped middle.* He read it four times but still wasn't sure what it meant. Other descriptions of sex acts made them sound absurd or painful. There was nobody to ask whether that was truth or part of the joke. He would sneak the book in and out of his room, and over again.

Books. Books had to be the answer. In the summer, Ali resolved to find something more helpful. Alone, he got on the District Line at Elm Park and an hour later emerged onto Tottenham Court Road. He entered a bookshop he had been to many times with his parents.

His heart beat through his T-shirt as he found the gay section. Book after outspoken book winked at him. Some educational, some soft porn. He didn't know where to start. His sweaty hand reached for one then pulled back. He glanced over both shoulders, bent down, made a choice, stood up. Then he saw her. Priya, a girl from school. She was not in his year but her brother was. How had an Indian girl from Dubai ended up at this bookstore at this very moment? He needed to vomit. Ali dropped the book on the floor and ran out of the shop. He kept running until he reached the park of Soho Square, a park he would come to know well years later. He sat on the ground and pulled clumps of grass out by the handful.

*

Ali cannot be aroused by Aiden Shaw's penis. Ali is aroused by Aiden Shaw's penis. He compares it to his own. No contest. Is that a problem? The real problem, he realises, is the magazine itself. He's never had something as unedited as this, and he doesn't know where to hide it. He has to get rid of it. He takes a final look.

*

After the bookshop Ali knew. He knew that there would be no help. Not for now. Not here. He decided that he would swallow it and keep it down. He would cover the offending bits of himself with gold pen.

He plastered his bedroom walls with pictures of delicate nineties starlets cut out of *Empire* magazine. Michelle Pfeiffer. Winona Ryder. The occasional Cindy Crawford. When he ran out of wall space, he hung more from the ceiling using Blu Tack and thread. Once, his friends discussed how they would all choose to die, if given a choice. He said, 'Suffocated underneath one hundred naked women.' He came home and lay in bed thinking about Michael's blue eyes.

Sometimes it was almost too much. To be drowning because of the rocks in his own pockets. He wanted so badly to empty them out, to hand them over to someone, anyone. But he could not bring himself to do it. He kept sinking.

One day he watched a film, *The Piano*. It managed to be a thing of beauty despite the endless snipping The Censors had had to do to protect Ali from Holly Hunter's nakedness. In the final scene, they are sailing away to a new life. Holly has her beloved piano thrown overboard. As it drops, she deliberately catches her foot in a rope. She is pulled into the sea, the piano dragging her to the bottom. There she floats above it, peacefully. She has chosen to die, unable to cope with her own silence. But then her face changes. She struggles. She kicks herself free. She swims upwards and breaks the surface of the water, coughing into the light. *What a death*, Holly's voiceover says, *what a chance!*

That was it. After darkness comes light. He would find his chance. He would keep this all hidden in the blackness of the sea, but then he would move to London and break the surface. Yes, that was it. He would move to London, break the surface, and be free.

*

Suddenly Ali has no idea what to do with this, his dirty magazine. For no good reason, he is too afraid to simply throw it away. It will be found. People will know. He takes it out to the back garden where his father's barbeque stands, left out from the weekend. He lifts the lid, the sun-scorched metal searing hot in his hand. He drops the magazine in. It is open to the page of the freaks. He pours on a little lighter fluid. Not necessary, perhaps, but he is taking no chances. He lights a match. Ali can hear his old Islamic Studies teacher saying flames consume all evil in the end.

As the paper burns he thinks of London. Of the liberation it will give him, he is sure of it. Away from black markers, away from scissors, away from teachers talking about burning. He does not know now, cannot know now, that only next year the internet will arrive in the UAE. Taken by surprise, The Censors will not work out how to control it at first. He will suddenly be able to search for Hung Italian Men *or* Brad Pitt Nude *when his parents are out. Nor can he know that a few years further on, porn will become so prevalent, so overbearing that millions of people, not just him, will spend millions of hours watching other people have sex. And some of those people will actually have to install software on their own computers to restrict their access to it. And he certainly cannot know that decades later people will complain not that the government is limiting the news they read, but that everyone can create their own news, and nobody will know what is true. Entire chapters will turn out to be false.*

No, Ali cannot know any of that now. For now, he just watches the fire slowly swallow Aiden Shaw's penis, and dreams of the uncensored life to come.

. . .

THE VERY BEST IS AVAILABLE TO ME

Deborah Green

G rooming is the cruel rupture of a person from their *self*. One gets lost. If it happens at a critically young developmental age, all sense of spaciousness is obliterated, absorbed in its black hole. It is almost impossible to realise who I could or would have been had this chronic interference not taken place.

*

As I write, the sunrise emerges. It is coming up to eight-thirty on a mid-December morning. I calculate almost thirty-eight Decembers since that man came into my life when I was five years old. That is over thirteen thousand times I have woken up locked in the confines of his warped reality of *who I am*. That is over thirteen thousand sunrises where I've lived in the conditioning submerged beneath the lies of an abuser.

My voice was silenced. I had not yet been allowed to fully experience *me*. Had not known the fundamental human right of the freedom to find out. I know only this one reality, and it is terrifying to break out of the mould. Because what will be left?

*

Last night I had the weirdest dream. As I move through the therapeutic process my dreams are revealing to me where the emotional charges are. As this bright December sunrise screams through my bedroom window I feel at once connected to truth, stronger than ever before, uplifted in this hopeful new reality that there is a new way emerging for me.

I am questioning my sexuality. Not: *am I straight*, but why am I attracted to the men that I am, and every time left bereft and hurting? Why do I fall for guys who treat me poorly? Where are the qualities of genuine respect and appreciation? Whose is this lie I am living?

Much is surfacing. Last night was the first time my psyche revealed to me a disturbing dream with my abuser as a point of erotic fascination. I woke up in a cold panic. This is what grooming looks like, marked on the soul of a fully fledged woman. For so many years, I had thought my abuser was my father, albeit a stepfather. I'd had his surname, was under his authority and, I'd actually thought, his care. But he was not a caregiver at all; he was a deeply disturbed man who had entered a vulnerable family and taken hold, because he liked little girls. Not *liked* in the beautiful sense of the word *appreciation*; rather, that he lusted after them and intended to shape their soft minds with his grooming; to censor them from the truth of who they were in order to control them. He succeeded: My sister and I, his prey.

*

THE VERY BEST IS AVAILABLE TO ME.

I am working this affirmation, this mantra. I tried one with the word 'deserve' in it, in a positive framing, but I could not get through the wall of what it meant, what to do with the word *deserve*.

*

My freedom was stolen. I should have received censor from harmful experience, as any child receives from a healthy adult. A normal person, instinctively, would never expose a child to inappropriate, damaging stories through television, movies, music, or direct conversation. *Parental Guidance* warnings appear to protect the vulnerable, but not in my childhood house; this has shaped my fundamental experience of what *love* and *care* are or can be.

So it is that as my forty-third birthday approaches this weekend, I'm stuck in a crappy bedsit in London and today I'm going out to seek a rich man for a paid encounter.

I reason to myself, *At least I'm going after big fish, not bottom feeders.*

It feels like I am walking a fine line between what I feel I can have and what I have been conditioned to believe about myself: *That I'm a worthless piece of shit.*

*

THE VERY BEST IS AVAILABLE TO ME.

I'm truly working with this in so very many moments each day. Last night in the yoga class, after not attending in over a month, a tear jewelled down my cheek as I felt once again in my happy place. I felt the liberation of self-care.

*

I figure, if I'm going to engage in sex work then the very best must be available to me. I have done the years of stripping, the complexities of having a sugar daddy when I was too immature to grasp what I was getting into, and I've done stripper-hoeing, where I've found my extra-curricular activities, handpicked from the club clientele. I look good, certainly for my age, but nonetheless, I am two decades older than a great many of the other dancers in strip clubs. That makes me feel foolish. Add to this how overcrowded (with girls) these clubs are, and the obscene fees clubs charge, and the imbalance there of the customers-to-dancers ratio and you see my dilemma. The last two clubs I danced in – after a year of trying to make a living wage as a yoga teacher – treated me terribly. On both counts I had to fight for my monies, which were initially withheld. These places are shit-storms. They weren't always like that, but they are now.

If I'm going to be a hooker then I'm going to find a person who pays well, who sets me on a new path. I am going to be with someone who is as generous and as healthy as possible within this framework. I know what I want and I know what must come next. In a way, I am looking for an angel investor. I may be deluded, but this is all I know; the way *I* know to go. Find the moneyman and give him honey-slam; it's deep in my programming. And until I know a better way, this is the only strategy I have: Use my pretty; use my charm. I am not entirely sure how men go about finding investment, but this much I know: Red lipstick is my PowerPoint presentation.

*

There is conditioning that happens epidemically at subtle as well as vulgar levels. In many ways, we are generations groomed to rate the female as a second-class citizen. Groomed to be second to males, through advertising and sexist storytelling in movies and on TV, and in the stories we act out with each other, handed down over the many years of patriarchy. Awakening is very much happening, and is vital, for the healthful evolution of all.

*

THE VERY BEST IS AVAILABLE TO ME.

Today I will go into the city. I will position myself in luxurious surroundings in Mayfair. I will wear my best coat and shoes. My nails are painted red. I will meet a lovely person who will give me lots of money. A man. I know how to play the game a man likes to play with a woman. I know the rules and can fashion the role. I do not particularly want to appear on a website for independent escorts. I need to freestyle, handpick. I will focus my mind on all the things I mean to manifest right away.

I will use this conditioning I have undergone to help me break away from it all. The same way that in order to remove a stain from fabric, with soap, you rub the stain against itself.

So now I appeal to the universe: Please help me get out of this spider's web. Send to me the person with whom I can heal some of this twisted reality. Somebody who will be fun and generous right from the start; somebody I can open the door with, to this new and bright future; somebody who is going to give me the genuine financial resources to do so; somebody who will leave as quickly as he arrived. I am ready.

To my inner child, at every age, I say this: You are perfect, untouched, untainted. The truth of who you are I know and God knows. This is between God and me now. I want you to feel assured that we are resolving this and bringing you into the light of truth. There are good people in this world. I walk in accordance with this truth from now on. From this moment forth I promise this is the case. *The very best is available to me.* The best of places, of opportunities and experiences is available to me.

*

So what now? I came into central London, not dressed

to kill, that would look too obvious; dressed looking like the author I wish to be; working at a piece like the author I wish to be. First stop, The Ritz. It's a saying isn't it – It's not The Ritz – to signify that one must know one's place. Well it was The Ritz, decorated for Christmas in such a way I gasped! I did not permit myself to stand and salivate at other people enjoying. I became other people, and I enjoyed. I did not spend a single penny but allowed myself to move about, used the beautiful powder room to check on my lipstick, listened to the pristine vocals of the choir at the piano, marvelled at the historic grandeur. All of these things I really like. It wasn't a place I could sit and write, so I moved along, and found myself at The Mayfair, at a table facing the street, and got myself a six-pounds latte. I have been here maybe two hours. All the while soaking up the atmosphere of success.

*

Censoring is not always a dirty word. It is a necessary part of our lives as social animals. Studies show the emergence in the brain of *shame* at age fifteen months. We need to accord, to appease our community, to fit in, for survival. It is important not to be an embarrassment. This is how it all ticks over nicely. This is the root of belonging, and it works.

For example, right now I am self-censoring appropriately. Whilst I am sitting at my MacBook, typing away like any other businessperson at this five-star hotel in one of the richest parts of London, I am behaving felicitously. Were I to be blatant and hustle the suits at their tables, well, I'd be breaking serious societal rules on decorum Shame has its regulatory and normal uses. Everybody who is here, having a posh experience, takes a dump every day, wakes up with bad breath and probably farts whilst asleep. Every manicured hand in here wiped a sticky bottom today, every shiny-shoed chap in here is also on his most respectable behaviour.

I have stayed here several times before, with the aforementioned sugar daddy. I loved staying here. I have eaten in this restaurant and even own the cookbook for it; that was twenty-five pounds, one of a great many lovely gifts from Robert. I had met Robert in a strip club in Liverpool, and for seven years, on and off, we pretended we had met in a regular bar, and I didn't have any economic need to work in clubs. Pretending is spiritually exhausting.

*

There is a scene here I witnessed. Independent escorts hang out in the bar. It is well known. A little scary to me, but maybe if I had discovered it when I was twenty-five years old, and could pull off a party dress and heels amongst other gals my own age, I could have got involved. Back then though, the early noughties, strip clubs were working pretty damn fine. Always made money. Always spent it as fast as I made it though; back to that word *deserve*, perhaps.

A red Ferrari just went past, a chauffeur-driven-whatever just slid up. Hallmarks of where I am. It gives me a thrill to be here. I have always liked the chase. Here I am looking like a real author, or a real businesswoman. Both of which, in a way, I am; I just don't have the outside evidence of this quite yet.

It is just that I have been blocked. Fear of humiliation can be very powerful. Whilst I have written children's stories, mostly I return to these themes of sex work, processing my experiences by recreating the same power dynamics as an adult. The difference being, I am an adult now, and as my dream revealed to me, I have humiliating contortions I can't even believe, and a lot of shame to unravel, despite my innocence.

*

It may be the case that I will close the laptop for the day, have a gin and tonic, and meet no one. That I take the red huff of night busses home, turn to my fridge for a supper. Honestly, the most important thing is that I am writing. After graduating from my degree in Imaginative Writing almost ten years ago, I wrote a novel. You can guess the themes. But I did very little to move it out into the world. I was morbidly ashamed of my themes. The truth is I am only just emerging from that. It is like I am getting born all over again. Still the tendrils or echoes of who I have been before, or rather, how I have felt before, move around me; but I am freer now than I feel I have ever been before. I am a liberated writer.

Can you imagine being a pianist, with a baby grand in your room, and having to walk past it every day for almost a decade, wondering the fuck how or when or if you will ever play again? This was extreme self-censoring, the kind that consumes you in its shame-hungry appetite. After all, nobody likes a whore do they?

But they should. I believe wholeheartedly in full decriminalisation of sex work, for safety, and because a person has the right to choose sex work without the evils of stigma, and because nobody gets to live on planet earth for free, and because it can be healing and it can be healthy. It is a complex matter but it cannot go unsaid. As long as the general consensus is that sex workers are bad women, it must be acknowledged that women are still hated, at a subtle level. Nobody is hating on the demand, though – the clients, typically men.

*

Why am I even here? Could I not get a normal job? And if not, why not? *A traumatised mind makes traumatised choices leading to traumatised outcomes*, my therapist had advised me when I berated the choices of an entire adulthood, in tears of anguish and dismay. Only this time, I don't intend the outcome to be a traumatic experience. And I need money. I am against the edges of my overdraft. Economics of living, even in a bedsit in London, are real and not radically different up north, where I am from. And you know what else? I want the very best, I want to go beyond the dusty windows, and this is all I know, this is my fucking programming. It's like a drug: just one more hit and I will get out. And I want the money fast, to help me move on. Even if I have been saying that for decades, I really mean it now.

*

I am feeling satisfied from writing. You can't imagine how peaceful I feel in the knowledge that I have been typing beautifully for hours, plus the scribing I did this morning; how warm and calm and authentic I feel, no matter the themes. In fact, I feel quite spent. That ride home with the home-cooked supper is almost as appealing as a dinner here and the trappings therein.

But. I'm broke. And I have made it this far. So I will go to the bar shortly, and be there for one drink on my own money, and just see, in that half-hour space, if anything floats to my island. And if nothing, I will sign up to the independent escort website tomorrow. It means getting a different phone number specifically for this kind of contact. I have taken advice from friends deep in the game. I know the steps. And maybe I will be back to The Mayfair soon, with a booking. Maybe that's the drill. And that's ok. It's ok.

*

I would like to give you the ending you want, because I know you are invested in this story now and want the heroine to have evolved by the end of it. An evolution into the very best, which *is* available to me.

. . .

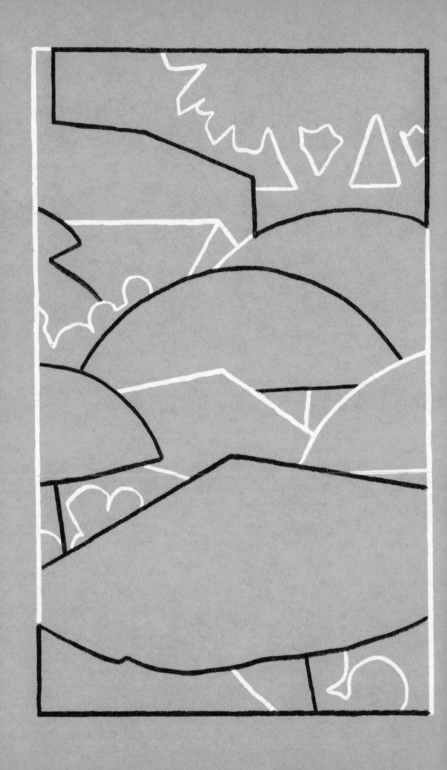

THE MANY DIFFERENT LIVES OF DENOLA

Timi Odueso

When we were children, our mothers told us to hold our ears open so their words could enter us easily.

We did not always want to listen. It was not often that we wished to sit under their watchful gazes and hear Denola's tale, and so we ran to the streams to bathe instead. We snuck out of open windows and found ourselves playing Suwe under mango trees, hoisting the limber ones up to fetch ripe fruits for us. When we burned soups, when our hands slipped and shards of broken clay pots scattered across the floor, we would quietly find our way to the farms, picking at cassava plants as fear grew in our hearts, for we knew that we would go to bed with palm-shaped stings on our backs and faces, our heads full of lessons we were supposed to imbibe from Denola's life.

When our own children came into the world and didn't wake early enough to fetch water from the taps of the towns we moved to, we began to remember the evenings we'd spent learning how to sing Denola's song. When angry farmers walked through our doors with empty baskets and claimed our children had roamed their fields and raped their maize stalks, roasting the cobs under makeshift grates they'd fashioned, our fingers itched as we remembered how our mothers had woven Denola into us. When the Ustazes that ran the Islamiyyas saw us at the markets as we haggled over the prices of yam tubers, as our fingers rummaged the velvety fabrics at the seamstresses', they asked us, with raised brows and snide voices, if we prayed five times daily, for our children forgot their verses so easily. Our palms would itch, in those delicate times, as we remembered how our own mothers had written Denola's fable into our creases with bamboo sticks. And so it came to be that we too began pulling our children by their ears as we sat them down between our thighs. We landed our palms on their faces and as they cried we began to weave Denola into the plaits on their heads.

Before we told her tale to our children, we unfurled the rolls of Denola's life amongst ourselves and we measured the fabric our mothers had shown to us; we laid the lessons across themselves and cut off the frayed edges. We said to ourselves, as we recited Denola's tale to our mirrors, 'Do you think this is fashionable today?' before we cut off the frills and bows which we were sure Denola would never again wear, were she alive. Where the colors of the tale had run pale over the years, we bought dyes of red and blue and dabbed over them, bright images that would burn into our children's faces. Where bits of wool had risen up against the fabric, we took out our knitting needles and picked them off. Where our mothers' version of Denola's tale was set at a time when there was an abundance of rain that wet the roofs and made the mud slippery, ours was set at a time when the sun shone menacingly upon the earth, drinking up the moisture with her heat and leaving Denola's town with nothing but thirst.

Our Denola had brown eyes and hair that always found new ways to wriggle out of the black wool her mother tied around it. Our Denola did not share a room with her three brothers, for in our version of her tale, which we whipped into our children, her father's farm yielded enough harvest for a house with corrugated-iron roofs that heated up the atmosphere of its six rooms in the day. She went to school with her younger brothers and came back to help her mother pound the yam while her brothers roamed the streets in search of fun. In our version of Denola's tale, everyone in the town kept empty drums under the gutters of their roofs every night in anticipation of rainfall; and in Denola's house, the task fell to her to ensure that the empty drums outside were stationed properly below the gutter and the full ones always had their lids wrapped tightly around their necks; for only she, of all her parents' offspring, had grown tall enough to see into the drums.

We watched our children keenly as we weighed their minds with Denola, we let our eyes catch the way their cheeks moved as we described Denola's village, the way their tongues moved to wet their lips when we told them of the thirst that ran through Denola's people, and when our children's voices rose up to say they had never heard of a child named Denola, when their eyes quivered with doubt as we told the tale of the town with no rain, when they raised their voices and said to us, 'Me, I've never seen any Demola before. Where did you say her house is?' We slapped their cheeks with our left hands and stuck fried beef into their mouths with our right hands.

This way, we slowly knit Denola into our children's lives, wielding, like our own mothers did too, fear in one hand and reward in the other.

'It wasn't always easy, you see,' we would say. 'When the drought came to suck the humidity away, Denola's blood had just began to show and so, she was easily tired and needed rest.' This was not the way our mothers told us of Denola's temper. To them, Denola was an unreasonable child; she began to grow angry at how much work she had to do, how she had to help her mother and clean up the house, how her fingers were always wounded by scalds from hot water as she turned the amala in the pot, or from hot oil as she fried the mackerels, how her brothers seemed to be able to do nothing else but eat and sleep. To our mothers, who pinched our nipples when they caught us playing with boys, the only explanation for Denola's action was the groundless disobedience that all children seemed to have.

When it was our turn to censor our children's behaviours with morals from Denola's life, we wove a little reason into Denola's anger and supported her behaviour with pillars moulded from common sense. As her tale reached the point when things began to break apart, we added fabric to the edges we found uneven, for we remembered the questions we couldn't ask our mothers and we knew our children's minds would wander in the same way ours had. So we told them of the female body and taught them of becoming.

'When you're a young girl whose body has just awoken, everything changes. Your body will always feel heavy, as if you have eaten too much garri. It will feel like everyone is against you and for six days every month, you will fight your body.'

'Then it's not really her fault, is it?' our children chorused. 'If she was sick, then they shouldn't have made her work.'

'But she wasn't sick. She was becoming a person, and sickness is not an excuse to disobey your parents,' we replied. We told them, after they broke plates they were supposed to be washing, of Denola's anger at everything and how her rebellion poisoned everything she knew and purged her family of what little liquids they had in their bodies.

Our children whispered amongst themselves with hands cupped around each other's ears. They twitched their eyes at one another and their cheeks swelled as they tried to swallow laughter. They turned to us with furrowed brows and scrunched noses, their lips quivering as they struggled to keep from falling into hysterics. 'But that's not possible. No one can suffer because children are disobedient. So you're telling us that if we don't listen to you, bad things will start happening to all of us?'

We watched their cynical faces with our noses turned up and our lips pressed tight as we shook our heads at their foolishness. We held bits of their skin between our thumbs and forefingers, pressing tightly, and as their screams rang out, we told them of the final moments of Denola's life.

'If she could, Denola would tell you to listen to us. If she could, she would tell you why,' we chastised. 'You remember it was one of Denola's chores to make sure the drums outside were fastened with lids before she went to bed? Well, Denola left them open one night, for she was angry that her mother had given her brothers the fish head at that night's dinner and when her father reminded her to check if the water drums were closed, she left his words at the dining table and went to bed. When she awoke the next morning, she found that the drums were still filled with water.'

Our children applauded and cheered on Denola; they looked up at us and said, 'You see, nothing happened. Those people had just been wasting that poor girl's time, making her do all that just for nothing. The water was still there.'

We flicked our fingers at their lips and told them to keep quiet. We told them they were impatient and stuffed into their palms slim shavings of roasted grasscutter. 'She fetched a few buckets from the drum and filled the basins in the kitchen and the bathroom. Her father took a cup and made his morning cornmeal and she watched her mother scold her brothers when they took too long bathing. Nothing happened till the next day when her father woke up too weak to raise his hands; he shivered under many wrappers and her mother boiled some water in a pot, and made a spicy pepper soup for him.'

We told our children how Denola was called to feed her father, how his teeth chattered as the spoon grazed his teeth. We told of how she woke up at night, and spooned some soup for herself, picking at the fish head with hungry fingers and throwing the bones into the latrine. We told of how Denola's mother, who had woken up in the middle of the night to relieve herself, found her husband's wrapper soaked in blood and his body unmoving. 'In a panic, she called for Denola but heard nothing through the house but a gurgling sound. She left her husband's body and dashed to Denola's room. Do you know what she found?'

When they shook their heads, we showed our teeth and said slowly, 'She found her daughter, choking on blood, jerking around like a chicken whose neck has just been sliced open. She yelled for the neighbors and they burst in and when they saw the blood gushing out of Denola, they held their noses and ran back the way they had come. When they came back with doctors in the morning, they found mother and daughter entwined in a pool of congealed blood. Their eyes were open and a trail of red was drawn around their mouths, their eyes, their noses and even their ears.'

'Why did that happen?' our children asked.

'It happened because Denola did not listen to her father. Her father had a farm and he knew that the drought affected animals as well as humans and he knew of the different diseases animals carry. The neighbors found, at the bottom of the drum outside Denola's house, a dead rat, swollen from its inebriation with water. Of how it had gotten in the drum, they had only one explanation: someone must have left the drums open.'

'Where is Denola now?'

Our mothers did not answer clearly when we too had

asked this question. They pointed at the stars and said to us, 'She is now up there, a star in the sky, lighting the correct path that all good children must take.'

For a few days after we had tightened the ends of Denola's tales on our children's heads, they would listen to everything we said. They would wake early and rush to taps; their lips would dance as they recited their verses and our glasses would be safe as they carefully washed the dishes, at least for a few days. When they burned too bright again, we tempered them with Denola's blood as we used her shame to douse their excess.

When their happiness made them float, we welded chains forged from Denola's gloom, and weighted them down with responsibility. When they faltered and reports got back to us that their behaviours had resurfaced, we censored their wrongs with lessons as we reminded them of Denola's failures.

And when they too grew up and found people with whom they could spend the rest of their lives, when their children sprang forth into the world and began to turn their backs on their parents' words, our children remembered the words we had carved into the marks on their faces. They sharpened their pencils, unfurled the scrolls upon which we had written Denola's tale and slowly, they too began to add new versions to the many different lives of Denola.

• • •

FICTION

THREE ACTS FROM A WOMAN'S LIFE

Mitra Teymoorian

Some moments are unforgettable.

The moment I realized I was all grown up

I was looking at myself in the mirror: cheeks round and white, a smile from ear to ear, two empty spaces instead of my two front teeth, a brand-new school uniform, and a white headscarf. Maybe I remember it so vividly because it was my first time wearing my school uniform. In one swift moment, I felt like I became a woman. In the schoolyard, when they sent me to the back of the line, I got a little cranky. But it was only because I was taller than all the other kids. There was a tiny little girl, standing in front of the line. It really bothered me that they would put her in front of the line, with that ridiculous look. My mom was standing by the wall, waving at me. It looked like she wanted to leave but didn't feel like she could. She told me, 'Pay attention!' by waving her arms and mouthing the words. That morning, on the way to school, she was asking me for the thousandth time: 'If they ask you if you have a cable dish at home, what do you say?'

I said, 'I will tell them that we don't.'

'If they ask you when you have guests at home, does your mother put on her veil, what do you say?'

I said, 'I will tell them that she does.' She thought I didn't get it. The day that I asked the neighbor's kid to pull down his pants so I could see what it looked like, and then my dad gave me a real good beating, I realized you can't tell everyone everything. I knew that the neighbors could not find out that we got our furniture from my dear auntie, the landlord could not find out that Dad got a raise, Grandma could not find out that Dad hit Mom, and Mom and Dad could not find out that a few nights ago, I saw them hugging in their bedroom. I was all grown up.

I was strong and naughty so the other kids respected me. Fereshteh – Angel – the tiny one from the front of the line, was one of those quiet ones, the total opposite of me. She was shy and afraid. The other kids teased her. I didn't like her very much, but since they had just moved to our neighborhood, and our moms became friends, we would walk to school and back home together. One day, she told me that the kids stopped teasing her once she started hanging out with me. Then she held my hand and laughed. That's the moment I started liking Fereshteh and thought that maybe I should always take care of her since she's so tiny. From then on we were best friends. It was a shame we weren't in the same class. Maybe if we had been, the classes wouldn't have been so boring.

One day I asked my brother, 'How many more days are left until the end of school?' He made calculations, then answered: 'One thousand, nine hundred and twenty days left until it's completely over.' I only knew how to count to one hundred, so I asked what that meant. He said: 'Until you become Uncle Reza's size.' Uncle Reza was very big. I lost all hope. I realized I could not be a good girl for all this time. To be honest, it would have been impossible.

One day, Fereshteh and I decided to pretend we had to go to the bathroom in the middle of class, then meet in the playground and play. My teacher had caught on that some kids were saying that they had to go to the bathroom when they really didn't have to go, so she said: 'If anyone lies about having to go to the bathroom, I can tell by looking into their eyes.' I got up and said: 'Ma'am, may I go to the bathroom?' The teacher came up to me, looked me straight in the eye and said: 'Do you need to use the bathroom?' I looked her back in her eyes as much as I could and said: 'Yes!' My teacher smiled and said: 'Go!' I was relieved to know that grownups are not as smart as they think they are. I ran to the playground and played until the end of the class, but Fereshteh didn't come. Her teacher found out she was lying. Fereshteh didn't know how to look straight into her teacher's eyes and tell her that she had to go to the bathroom.

The moment I realized happiness is near

My heart was pounding. For the past twelve days, I had been checking the webpage every day to see the results of the university entrance exam, but they were not up yet. I was thinking of alternative plans. I clearly remember the sound of my sister pouring tea for herself and the smell of bread. My name showed up on the webpage, my registration number, then my father's name, and then the name of the college and my preferred subject. For one second, I felt as if blood wasn't reaching my brain. I started to scream. My mom jumped out of the bathroom. She thought there was an earthquake. After we experienced our first earthquake, she thought everything was an earthquake. Once she found out I'd been accepted into college, she realized that she was still wearing her bathroom slippers and started cursing at me for scaring her. After she washed the floor, she remembered to ask me what subject I was accepted into. 'Physical Education with a spot on the kickboxing team.' My mom was shocked.

'Did you even apply for Physical Education?' I completely forgot that I had not told them. Since I was a little girl, my mom always called me 'Doctor'. It wasn't even important to her that, other than PE, all my grades were horrible. She did what she wanted. My mom said, with a sad tone, 'Wait until your father comes home to see if he even lets you study PE, before getting too excited.'

I immediately replied: 'If he doesn't let me, I will run away.'

Suddenly my cheek was burning from the slap my mom gave me, and then she started to cry. I didn't even care. I had grown thick skin by now. As soon as I saw that I was accepted into college, I envisioned myself getting a gold medal in an international arena. If my mom was nicer, I'm sure I would have included her in my 'thank you' speech during the receipt of the medal. It's a shame she isn't. While she was blowing her nose, she complained, 'Your poor father runs around all day long like a dog. At his age, he needs to put up his feet and rest, but instead, he works as a driver so that he can pay for your studies, and you are so ungrateful.'

I couldn't hold it in any longer: 'Who asked you guys to have kids?' My mom got mad again. I escaped and ran out to the fire escape and climbed up to the roof. I knew she couldn't climb the fire escape due to her bad knee. She kept cursing and complaining from downstairs anyway. I really didn't care. I yelled down at her: 'I was accepted to a prime college and this is how you thank me?' A sandal flew up, and with it, my mom's words: 'You'll eventually have to come down!' I didn't pay attention to her. She kept wailing, 'It was my fault for letting you go to the boxing club without telling your father. I thought if you got punched a couple of times, you would get over the love of boxing.' I lay down on the roof without a care. The fall air was so nice. I wanted to lie right there all night long and watch the leaves move around in the trees. I heard the kids playing on the street, yelling very bad words at each other. I heard the donkey owner selling onions and the neighborhood wives nickel and diming him. I closed my eyes and started fantasizing. I would become rich and leave this neighborhood. I would move uptown. Wasn't it the Judo sisters who became street vendors, and now they are rich? Nowadays the champions have it worse than the rich, lazy kids. I took my cigarettes out from between the tiles and went closer to Fereshteh's rooftop so that mom didn't notice the cigarette smell. Fereshteh hadn't come up yet. Earlier, we had agreed that as soon as she found out her results, she would come upstairs, but there were no signs of her. I lit my cigarette and took my first puff. Then I went back into fantasyland. I'm standing on top of the podium and biting my medal. I'm dying to bite my medal. Fereshteh is sitting in the audience. I look at her and punch my chest twice. At that moment, the door opened and Fereshteh came up. She gave me a big smile so that I knew everything was fine. She removed her veil and spun it in the air. Her bright red veil in the middle of a bunch of gray buildings and the leaves on the oak trees that were shaking and changing from gray into green colors became that unforgettable moment.

The moment I realized I'd lost everything

Until I grow old, I'll never forget these white walls, the quiet nurses, and the smell of the hospital.

I go to her room, but do not go inside. I don't have the courage to see her. Last night I saw the pictures of her on Instagram. She was completely covered in bandages. How do I even know that this is Fereshteh? I saw that my sister was crying. I got up, got dressed and went to the hospital. It was late. In front of the hospital, I sat on the steps of a house and watched the hospital windows. This wasn't supposed to happen. We had so many plans. I had promised her I would get her out of this damn country. We would go somewhere where nobody would bother us. I'd buy a nice house. I'd bring home a cute cat or dog, whatever she wants. She promised me she wouldn't hurt herself again. I didn't think she would break her promise, but I didn't realize how fed up she was. Her life was a constant war: studying, working, getting dressed, watching soccer, falling in love. In all of it, she struggled against standards. With a dad who was a mini-dictator of the house, a mom who cared more about what other people thought, and people who judged her. Fereshteh was tiny, never a bully, and worst of all, she didn't know how to lie.

Her mom and dad are in the room. If they see me, they will make a scene. They will be able to see everything through my eyes. All parents want to put the blame on someone else. Actually, this time they wouldn't be wrong. Even I know that it's my fault. That's why I don't have the courage to enter the room. If it wasn't for me encouraging her, Fereshteh isn't someone who would ever dress in men's clothes and go to the stadium. At first, it was a joke. We wrapped our chests in bandages. I was fine, but it didn't matter how hard Fereshteh wrapped her chest, because if you got close enough to touch her, you could tell she's a girl. In the chaos of the stadium, everyone was stuck to each other. Eventually, someone found out and told on her. The jerk who pushed himself on her and made comments to her made my blood boil, and I punched him in the eye. It's true that I'm a kickboxing champion, but I know that when I hit a man, I have to run away from there as soon as I can because I wouldn't be able to handle several men by myself. The worst part was that Fereshteh wasn't a fast runner. I'm such an idiot. I knew she's not a fast runner but had to bring her there anyway. I told her to run, and I ran too. I didn't look back. Fereshteh got caught. I have to give it to her that she didn't rat me out, but I wish she had; then it wouldn't hurt so much. However, we both knew that if I got caught, it would be very bad for me. I could either be suspended from the games or be punished in another way. Maybe that was in the back of my head when I ran and didn't look back.

As soon as I arrived home, I went on the rooftop and stared at her front door until the middle of the night. I was nauseous from worrying. Her phone was still off. I sent my sister to her house. Her mom had said: 'I know who tricked her because my daughter would never do something like this on her own. Now they have let her out until her court date.' *Court date?* What did she even do? I thought they would get her statement and let her go, but court is too much for something small like this. Her dad said: 'Who will marry my daughter if she has a record?' Good! I hope no one proposes to her.

I couldn't see Fereshteh at all. She even stopped giving

the stray cats from the neighborhood food at night. I would go to practice all day long and sit on the rooftop, staring at her rooftop every night. Then she went to court. I thought they would scare her a little bit and let her go, but I don't know who told her in court that she would get a six-month sentence. *Six months?* Did we steal something? When they got back home, her dad threw her in the room, locked the door and left. Then her mom smelled smoke and tried opening the door, and saw that it was locked. She ran into the street and told the neighbors, who broke the door down. I was in the ring when this happened. Fereshteh was always on my mind. I was sick to my stomach. I was mad at myself, at the soccer federation, at the lawmakers, and at the ones who enforce the rules. I was going crazy until suddenly a few people jumped me and held my hands and feet. My opponent was on the ground, in a pile of blood. I almost killed her. My coach told me to go home and wait for the disciplinary committee to come. I came home and heard what she had done to herself. If it was me, I would have poured gas on everyone else and would have set them on fire, but Fereshteh was different from me. She was good. Why the hell do I say *was*, she still *is*. I miss her and her laughter a lot. Whenever I was fed up with everything, only she could make me laugh. Anything that happened to me, she was the first to know.

I hear the voice of the soccer narrator. They are showing soccer on the TV in the waiting room of the hospital. A bunch of men gathered around watching. I go straight in the middle; it's not theirs! I hope Fereshteh has a TV in her room. This game is very important to us. We were supposed to watch it together. We even made a bet. Fereshteh said that our team captain would score the first goal in the first half of the game, and I said that we would score the first goal in the second half of the game. The team is playing well. I don't want to watch it by myself. I go to the end of the hallway. I wish I could see her so I could tell her: 'Just get better, and I'll take you anywhere you want in the world to get plastic surgery, and you'll look even better than the day you were born. Then we will live somewhere where we can go to the stadium and watch the games. We might even play. Just like when we were kids, and we would play on the street. You will be the goalie and I'll be the striker. You will protect the goal with your life, and I will kick holes into the goal. Just like the time we were eight years old, and you threw yourself so hard to the ground that you broke your arm. But you caught the ball. Do you remember how much you would laugh and upset the boys? I hear the men screaming, and I remember the game is on. We scored. I step up. The captain scored. I don't know why I start to tear up. I'm not the kind of person who cries over silly things like this. I just wish you could see that you won the bet. You guessed right like you always do.

'Within an hour, you died and you didn't even realize you won the bet. You never saw the rest of the game, the beautiful house, and the cute cat. You never saw me bite my medal, punch myself twice in the chest and point at you.'

What am I going to do with this sorrow for the rest of my life?

• • •

//AUTHOR'S NOTE//

In Iran it is illegal to use cable TV to watch foreign channels, and women must wear a hijab in front of everyone other than husbands, brothers or sons. If they do not, they can be punished.

THE GENERAL AND THE BIRDS

Fernando A. Torres

---

aughtily, proudly and almost valiantly, the General began his one-block, slow march towards the small flowery park, flanked by a ridiculous procession of bodyguards, bootlickers and their tasteless wives. The hot morning sun of the pampas scurried behind a cloud, as if embarrassed by the scene, making the entourage's shadows disappear from the hot, dark stretch of pavement. Once in the park, the General and a sprinkling of officials sat on big colonial chairs borrowed from the dusty downtown Museum of History. The proscenium was small: to his right his wife and to his left the governor of the province, another high-ranking military officer appointed to the post by one of the General's busy fingers. Next to the governor sat the chief of the political police, wearing dark sunglasses that made him look – perhaps on purpose – like an owl.

Nobody noticed a few tiny birds lying dead on the side of the stage except for Damián, one of the musicians forced to appear before the General, who stood staring at the feathered corpses. Damián was the first in line of the musical ensemble, a guitar hanging from his neck and a long, dark, Spanish Batman-style cape draped around his shoulders. His face attracted the attention of the audience, which gradually became aware of the awkwardness surrounding the lifeless creatures. Later on, the truth would come out: the little birds had committed suicide.

Damián was part of La Estudiantina, an acoustic ensemble of university students performing traditional Spanish love songs. The student musicians were 'persuaded' by the university officials to 'voluntarily' serenade the General. Fearful of losing their tuition and being expelled from school, most of the students agreed to perform. And perform they did, but, in an act of audacious rebellion, they all decided to de-tune the instruments right before their appearance. For a musician, playing out of tune is like painting in the rain for a painter. It is an unforgivable act of negligence and lack of professionalism with an incalculable cost to their reputation. What a mutinous act! An insult to everybody's ears! The serenade – which, of course, sounded horrible – brought a uniform, devilish smile to the students' faces.

The solitary poet in attendance, Evaristo, also 'cordially' invited to declaim a few verses for the General, was inspired to stutter – perhaps on purpose – 'The Fall', a two-minute anonymous poem that nobody understood. Evaristo, who was also an actor, performed the stutter so well that the public instantly felt sorry for him. The uncomfortable General crossed and uncrossed his legs several times. 'The Fall' is a seventeenth-century poem about a beautiful flower that chooses to die rather than welcome the brutal winter. What a mutinous act!

All those attending the public meeting to welcome the General seemed uneasy. The teachers, afraid of losing their jobs, brought their students. Everything proceeded like a regular military event until the General suddenly lowered his head, hiding his reddened face, apparently in anger. He had noticed a large wall facing the park and painted with political slogans, one of them openly calling for his overthrow: 'Our song is none other than everybody's song.'

Thenceforth, the General and his government of the closure the local conservatory of music, ordered the guitars and poetry books burned, banned the use of certain musical keys except those used by the Prussian military brass bands, and suspended poetry and all other insubordinate literary endeavours. Ultimately, the General ordered that all the birds of the pampas be shot, but his troops, stupidly, forgot to search the nests — perhaps on purpose — but I doubt that.

· · ·

//AUTHOR'S NOTE//

Decades after Pinochet's public appearance at the Parque Japonés in the city of Antofagasta, Damián told me in an almost apologetic way how little recollection he has of the event's details. The only thing he remembers vividly was seeing a couple of dead sparrows at his feet, like a pre-monition of something, he said. Birds also suffered the military's dull-witted methods of problem solving: in the highlands, the endangered parinas, or pink flamingos, were a favourite salty dish in the military encampments, and turkey vultures were shot by festive military patrols to oust them from the city's downtown square.

THE SONG BIRD

Nathan Alling Long

Her boyfriend once told her that with practice she could learn to sing, which was his way of saying that she could not sing at all. He was a composer, so he should know. He was also rather demanding of beauty in general, so it was not a surprise that he would say such a thing. Still, it hurt. She had always believed she could sing, particularly to the rhythm of water in the shower tapping against her body.

He had later said that he was surprised by her voice: she was so beautiful, he had expected her voice to be as beautiful. It was a fault of his, he said, to make such assumptions about people, as though such a confession would make her feel better about his comment.

She did not want to take lessons – she didn't have the money or the patience. Instead, she took what money she had and bought a songbird that someone moving to another country was selling. She took it for many reasons, each one more private and personal than the last. One was because she felt badly for a creature abandoned by its owner. Two, she imagined the songbird might sing while her boyfriend worked on his compositions, annoying him now and then. Three, she thought the bird might sing for her, be her voice in that small two-room apartment they shared, where she had taken mostly to reading books and sweeping the old wooden floors meticulously every morning. And four – well, four was so private and unimaginable that she kept it all to herself.

At first, her boyfriend was charmed by the songbird. He even incorporated some of the tiny phrases the bird sang into his compositions. 'It's like my muse,' he said to her one night at the dinner table. This made her sad, for she thought she was his muse. He had even told her that once, when he'd asked her to move in with him. Had he forgotten?

As the months passed, the boyfriend gradually tired of the songbird. 'Shhhh!' he would hiss at it as he worked at his piano, and after it had interrupted him too often, he would get up and put the cloth over the bird's cage to make it think it was night, which would silence it.

'I thought it was your muse,' she said one afternoon after he had covered the cage.

'It was,' he said, 'but it keeps singing the same notes, or else it just imitates what I've just played on the piano. I can't move forward.'

She nodded and went back to her book. At times it was hard for her to read with the random tinkling of the piano keys, the same three or four notes played over and over, with a slight variation or a chord thrown in. Those times, she wished she could have thrown a cloth over him and his piano so she could concentrate on her book. But it was his apartment, and this was his work.

Soon, the songbird was covered up much of the day and night, because the city lights were bright enough at night that it would sing and keep them up if the cage was uncovered while they slept.

On days the boyfriend was gone, she would tear off the cloth and sometimes even let the bird fly free in the apartment. It would flutter and squawk, then perch on the floor lamp and sing and sing.

'I know how you feel,' she would say, and sometimes she would sing along with it, her own song, not caring how much the two melodies clashed or how off-key she sang. But then the boyfriend would come home, the songbird would go back in the cage, and if he needed to work, the cloth would be placed back over it.

One night, the boyfriend announced to her that he had an important new commission. It would mean a lot of work at home, but when it was done, he would have his piece performed by the Tokyo Philharmonic.

'That's very exciting,' she said.

'It is,' he said. He had brought a bottle of champagne to celebrate. 'But I'll need to work in the apartment, need for it to be quiet.'

'Aren't I quiet enough?'

'What?' he said. 'Oh yes. I wasn't talking about you.' He took a sip of champagne. 'You are always quiet enough. And I appreciate that.'

She smiled.

He looked back and smiled flatly at her. 'But the bird makes lot of noise. I feel badly keeping it in the dark all day and night.'

'I see,' she said. She understood that this was his way of saying that the songbird had to go. She wondered if he really felt badly for the bird at all.

She didn't talk the rest of the meal, but that was not unusual for her. They often ate in silence. Her boyfriend liked it that way, because he said he found inspiration from the random noises of the city – a horn, a car alarm, the gunning of an engine, a phrase shouted from the street in some other language. Though the songbird was not covered, it did not sing at all, as though it were listening to the couple, sensing its fate was being decided.

Over the next few days, she considered what to do. She did not want to abandon the bird as the previous owner had. And it was the only thing she had, beside her books. And though they could talk to her, they could not sing to her. She did not have a job or another place to live, so she could not simply abandon her boyfriend. Plus, there was something exciting about his rise to fame. She was proud of him, and more than that, the commission made her feel that she was still his muse, especially now that it was clear the songbird was not.

In the end, she decided to do with the bird what she had most secretly wanted to do when she had bought him from the man – her fourth reason. She would swallow the bird whole and let it live within her.

She first had to talk to the bird, hold it in her hand and explain the situation. She knew this plan wouldn't work unless it agreed to cooperate. She explained the importance of this new piece of music her boyfriend was writing and the alternatives she had to swallowing the songbird. She asked the bird if it was willing to live inside her. She explained that it would be dark all the time, but that she would keep it safe and hoped that, despite the darkness, it would sing to her now and then.

The songbird tilted its head, as though trying to understand this strange and unbird-like request. But then it looked into her eyes and gave her a tiny nod.

She smiled as her tears fell. She coated its wings in oil so it would slip down her throat more easily, then she opened her mouth wide – as though she were singing a libretto or about to scream – and tilted her head back.

The songbird slid down easily and landed in her belly,

causing a few sharp pains where its claws grabbed at the lining of her stomach. 'There,' she said to the bird, and she felt it flap its wings as far as they would go and then settle down.

That night the boyfriend came home and noticed the bird was gone.

'Thank you,' he said, though he didn't ask what she had done with it. 'This will make work so much easier.'

She smiled, her secret sealed within her.

'I guess we can get rid of the cage,' her boyfriend said, 'now that the bird is gone.'

'No,' she said. 'The cage stays.' She wanted something in the apartment to remind him that it had once been there.

'But we have so little room.'

'I took care of the bird. The cage won't make a sound.'

He looked at her. She did not budge. 'I guess it's not in the way,' he said.

Over the following weeks, she realized that keeping a bird inside her took more work than she imagined. First, she had to eat birdseed daily, and eventually the bird asked her if she might not give it a worm now and then? The idea disgusted her, but she cared for the songbird so much, she began digging up worms in the grass behind the apartment and swallowing them whole. Then the bird asked if it might have a perch to rest on so that it did not have to keep its feet in the muck of the food she ate. This too seemed impossible, but she understood the need and decided to figure a way to accommodate it. She could not swallow a branch, let alone a whole tree so, instead, she swallowed some seeds. But after several weeks, they did not grow, so she swallowed a tiny sapling, its roots planted in mud, and that fixed itself to her stomach and survived.

The songbird then told her that it and the sapling needed sunlight to grow, and so she had to figure out how to get daylight to the bird and its tree. This was more difficult. She could not take a handful of sun and swallow it. She could not build a sun within her. She puzzled over this for several weeks, all while her boyfriend wrote his symphony. Finally, she decided to make a small incision in her belly to let the light in. She could not do this at home, since her boyfriend worked by the window and would be disturbed, so she took a kitchen knife and went to the city park where she found a patch of sun within a circle of bushes. There, she lay on the ground, sliced open her belly, and pulled apart the flesh until sunlight poured into her stomach. She lay at just the right angle so that the songbird and tree got light. And from her belly, beautiful songs began to emerge, songs she had never heard before. For the bird understood what sacrifices she made to care for it, and the songs were no longer sung out of habit or boredom, but out of love.

Though it was painful to pull open the wound every day, the music that rose from her body was so beautiful it pushed the pain away. She began to spend more and more time in the park, longing for those quiet hours lying on the grass in her private spot, the pain and music trembling from her body.

Her boyfriend was working so hard on his composition, he didn't notice how often she was away from the apartment. They had not made love for several months, but one night, after a day of frustration over the final movement, he began to touch her. He felt the wound on her belly and pulled back, his hand wet with blood.

'What is that?' he said. 'What happened?'

'I cut myself making dinner,' she said calmly. She felt the soft, feathered head of the songbird caress the inside of her belly.

'Let me see; it feels so deep.'

'It's fine,' she said. 'Let's just go to sleep.'

'Shouldn't you see a doctor?'

'I'll be fine,' she said. 'You need rest to finish your work.'

The next morning, the boyfriend returned to his symphony, and she went off to the park. It was overcast, but she knew that there is a great deal of sunlight even on a cloudy day. She lay in her protected spot, pulled open her wound and positioned her body so that the light could get in.

The songbird began to flutter and sing. The song was so beautiful, she wept as she lay on the ground. Soon, she heard footsteps nearby and realized that people had gathered around the bushes to hear the bird. At first, she feared they would come into the crown of bushes and discover her, but then she realized they were keeping a distance, perhaps so as not to frighten the bird.

She lay like that for hours, her wound exposed to the cloudy sky, the songbird singing, the silent crowd of people circling her, listening to its song.

She did not leave the park until night, when the light had left the sky, the bird had stopped singing, and the people had dispersed. She came home, but her boyfriend was gone, crumpled sheets of staff paper scattered around the piano. She went to bed. Her boyfriend came home hours later, knocking into things and swearing in the dark. He fell asleep beside her as she held her wound together and breathed.

The next few days, she took a rest from the park and read her books on the couch. The long day had exhausted her, and her wound did not heal like it had before. She felt something pressing against her stomach from inside, and the bird let her know that the tree had grown with all the sunlight and water it had received.

Her boyfriend returned to composing, seeming to have overcome his impasse. Perhaps she really was his muse. At dinner, he told her he was almost done with the symphony.

'Congratulations,' she said, though the pressure in her stomach was so great she could barely eat.

He asked how her wound was healing, and she said, 'Fine.'

'But it's swollen,' he said, suddenly seeing her belly.

'Is it?' she said.

'Are you pregnant?' he asked.

'No,' she said, though she felt it was a lie, for she did have a creature inside her, one that she loved. The songbird was like a baby to her.

'I don't believe you,' he said. 'All this time, I've been working to earn what we need, and you go get knocked up by someone.'

'No,' she said.

But he was so angry, he could not hear it. 'Just get out.'

'But I have nowhere to go.'

'Go to him.'

'There is no him,' she whispered, but felt too ill to fight. She left the apartment and went to the only place she knew. In the bushes, she lay down, trying to sleep under the bright, full moon. She couldn't sleep and felt so lonely. She wanted the songbird to sing, but he never sang in the dark.

Would you like moonlight? she finally asked the bird.

What is that? the songbird said.

It's sunlight reflected off a planet in the sky.

That sounds beautiful, it said.

It is, she replied. She unbuttoned her shirt and pulled open the wound. It had barely healed, and the sides came apart easily in her hands. She saw a branch unfold from her belly and reach toward the moon. Then the songbird hopped out onto the branch and gazed up into the sky. It began to sing as she lay on the earth and closed her eyes.

In the months that followed, in that place surrounded by bushes, the tree grew tall, and the songbird made a home in its branches. It sang every night. Many people came from across the city to hear it. But not the boyfriend, who stayed in his apartment, working on the final movement of his symphony, though he never quite found the right notes for its end.

• • •

VESTIGES

Kiki Gonglewski

The first time I saw her she was sitting in the
corner of I–95, ever so slightly removed from
the quotidian. Knees pulled to her chest, she
was peering intently at something held delicately behind
cupped hands. I don't know why I walked over to her. I
still had other areas of the main hallway to clear. I usually
saved enclaves like the one she was currently occupying
until the last part of my shift. Sweeping up against the
corners of the walls first, where the austere metal met
concrete, before doubling back to catch any sequestered,
stray litter. She was dressed in the same gray jumpsuit as
everyone else, and none of her features were particularly

striking. But there was something about that downward gaze, so utterly engrossed in her hidden treasure... it made her shine like nobody else. I began to gently push through the crowd, foraging restlessly from one nowhere to the next. No one paid me any mind other than a few dime-store utterances of annoyance if they accidentally jostled me or ran into my collection cart. I noticed, while trying to keep my head above water, that there was something of a smile playing about her face. Faint, shifting under the occasional florescent flicker of lights, so that I was not entirely sure if it was actually there from one moment to the next. Her fingers moved occasionally, as if she were fiddling with something. I had to see the secret nestled behind those fingers.

As I made my way through the traffic of people to which the passage of I-95 owed its inspired nickname, the flutter of their gray fabric clothing sometimes obscured my view of her. I was afraid the next time my eyes found their way back to that spot she'd be gone before I had a chance to see what she was holding. I could see that it was some kind of paper, small, peculiar-looking. Crumpled up and folded into some odd shape. Why? Paper only existed for brief periods at a time before being pulped again. No one was supposed to hold onto it.

Now standing beside her, I followed her gaze down into her cupped palms. She was holding the beige, slightly ridged material of our milk cartons. Corners meeting others to show a white underbelly in certain places, lines meeting one after another to form triangles and squares in three dimensions.

I cleared my throat a little sheepishly to get her attention. 'Detritus,' I murmured, and extended a hand.

At the sound of my voice, the woman's head jerked up in vague surprise, as if she had just been abruptly woken up from some inopportune but pleasant dream. Her mouth was slightly ajar still, eyes beautifully wide. Then, within a few moments her expression subdued slightly, its brightness fading, returning to contours of neutrality and the realization that I was still waiting. She gave me a slight nod and handed the crumpled carton over, placing it gently on the palm of my outstretched hand. It balanced there, like some little creature, teetering uncertainly on its four small triangular feet.

'Thanks,' I muttered. *Stupid. What a stupid thing to say.* Then, as a bit of a shy afterthought, I added, 'I'm sorry, miss.'

'You're okay,' she said in response, before her gaze, no longer fixated by her creation, was swept out to the river of people and, I somehow suspected, far beyond...

I quickly turned my back to her and began busying myself with the edges and corners of things again, and a few more items of debris that ended up along them before being tossed into my collection cart.

There weren't any windows along I–95, or anywhere for that matter. No decorations. Nothing distracting. Nothing extra. Only the scant fundamentals necessary to retain efficiency and sustain life. I don't know what all those people did in their identical gray jumpsuits as the river swept them upstream to their jobs and back home again. Or rather, rush hour was the proper, local term for the morning and midday bustle. No one else spoke of rivers. It must have been something to sustain the system too, I suppose. As a janitor, all I knew was how to collect and sort out detritus, classified as non-government allocated possessions, anything and everything past immediate practical use, for reuse. This included the obsolete curiosities people sometimes hid in their homes. No room for them anymore. We lived in a zero-waste society. So, every week, we were assigned to random residential searches. Jewelry, art, maps of places and cities that no longer existed, non-allocated paper, old clothing, obsolete filmstrips, and books. Sometimes I didn't even know what it was that I was handling, what it was that I was getting rid of. But I didn't really need to know in order to do my work. I could recognize Old-World relics when I saw them. All of them had to be taken away, ushered into new lives as clothing, food cartons, or sleeping amenities for the masses. And the transactions were always accompanied by that wide-eyed stare of their desperate former owners. Not her, though. There was a soft, far-off kindness about her eyes, without any anger or fear or indignation. But they were the ones that followed me into my dreams along with that funny little milk-carton creature that tossed its head about and reared up excitedly on its hind triangular legs before galloping clumsily towards me.

'Detritus,' I mumbled. 'Sorry, miss.'

The woman gave me a brief smile, mirthless though definitely not unkind, and handed over a plump-looking green critter with two long limbs flanking both sides of its body and a triangular snout. I'd been doing this for a little over a week, now. She'd been coming to the same spot like clockwork at around one in the afternoon with scrap papers from her job or trash from lunch and working on her creatures during her mid-day break. Perhaps it was the puzzle that hooked me. What she did, whatever that was, she did in plain sight. She knew what would happen. She knew someone would take her creation away. Yet that didn't seem to deter her. I always wanted to say something more to her, but never found the right words. She probably hated me anyway. After all, I was always the one conspicuously going out of his way to swoop by and take her children away. Like clockwork.

'You're okay,' she responded.

'Just the rules,' I murmured pathetically, looking down at her latest construction. 'It's…pretty, though.'

'Ah, well,' she sighed, her head gracefully tilted slightly upwards as she followed the line between the gray wall and austere ceiling, like where the sky meets the sea at the horizon-line. Or so I'd heard. 'You're only doing your job. There isn't much room for pretty things here anyway.'

I sat down next to her, back against the wall, throwing

her a skeptical side-glance. It lingered on her a little longer than I'd liked to have admitted. 'I really don't think that's quite true,' I laughed, and was rewarded with another ephemeral smile, along with those mesmerizing twin flashes of horizontal green that peeked out from under her thick lashes.

I turned the paper creature over. 'Why doesn't this one stand up like the others?'

'I always have a harder time making penguins cooperate than the others,' she laughed. 'I'll make you a better one tomorrow.'

I turned the thing over in my hand again until it lay on its back nestled snugly in my palms. 'Is this thing…a penguins?' I breathed in awe.

The woman laughed harder. 'Yes, it's called a penguin. It's an animal, a bird. It lives in the ocean.'

'The ocean…' I echoed softly, plinking one of its long limbs gently with my pinky finger. 'But can't it fly?'

'Yes. But it flies underwater,' she responded.

I couldn't help but snicker at this. 'How is that even possible?'

'I don't know. My grandmother taught me how to make these. And that's just what she told me.'

'And do you believe her?' I asked.

She grinned, letting her mind wander beyond the constricting walls surrounding her. 'Sometimes. On good days I do, at least. But either way, I believe in what she taught me.'

And I held the paper bird tighter in my hands.

I had caught a few pages of a book once, by sheer accident. It had belonged to a rather elderly man who'd stupidly been keeping it tucked away under his mattress. Afterwards, I was just rifling carelessly through the pages when my eyes hooked onto the edge of an indented paragraph like a fish on a line, and they cascaded down the pages pulled by some irresistible magnetism that I had never felt before, or would feel since. By the end of it, I'd lost control of my digits. They greedily flipped the pages of their own accord for several minutes before I managed to shut the thing in fear of being caught. The book had something to do with the sea… I'd never seen it before in real life. But since then, its impressions and rhythms kept me company through my monochrome days and slipped into my head at night.

A penguin. A peculiar bird that flew underwater. Back in my room, I murmured its name until I fell asleep…

'Detritus, miss. You know I would let you keep it if I could.'

'You're okay.'

I looked down at what she made. A little chubby-looking square with two very long, slender, funny-looking ears poking backwards out of its head. There was a random raid scheduled for this afternoon, someone on the watch list with a long history of anomalous behavior and three relocations in the last five years who had apparently fallen under suspicion once again. But I had my friend Greyson cover for me, coaxing him with promises of an exciting arrest. All so I could see this weird paper creature with the funny ears. Even if it was just for a few minutes...

I felt my throat tightening. 'I'm so sorry we have to throw them all away.' Her grandmother and her creations had no place here. They briefly bloomed into life only to be crushed by machines or trampled by people in gray jumpsuits. Little animals or books and the used Kleenexes or greasy wrappers of the world were all the same to the government. All trash to be reused, trash to be recycled, trash to denature, to de-soul in this heartless era where somewhere along the line, living had been thrown to the wayside in favor of surviving. 'Detritus. It's the rules. Detritus, you know... We have to throw everything non-essential, everything... everything out until there's nothing left of them at all, and...' I trailed off and looked at her hopelessly, only to be met with another radiant grin.

'Oh, I would just *love* to see you try,' she rejoined.

'What...what do you mean?'

Slowly, she took my hand in hers, taking the paper back from me. 'This is a rabbit.'

I looked over at her a little nervously. 'Okay.'

'And yesterday, as you know, I made a penguin.'

She pressed the rabbit flat and unfolded its nose.

'The day before that, it was a frog.'

She lifted its ears and smoothed them into oblivion.

'Then, a lion.'

The body was just squares with creases now, only a few hard folds separating it from its virgin paper-waste state.

'A kangaroo.'

Then, slowly, she began folding them again. I watched her fingers move.

'Then, before that I think... a sea turtle, a crane...'

By the time she finished, I was only dimly conscious of the fact that my mouth was ajar. I had never seen anything so mesmeric, so close to magic.

'Can you remember that?' She asked me softly, as if trying to gently tug my mind back to earth.

'What?'

'Can you remember all of the names of the animals?'

'Yes,' I breathed, realization rushing toward me like a tidal wave, 'of course...'

'Now, then.' She handed me back the rabbit, whole again. 'You gotta do what you gotta do.' Here, she gave me a wink. 'Detritus.'

I had started to measure all of time through her creations. Before her, the days melded endlessly into each other in blurry streaks of gray, only separated by the brief interims of sleep's dreamless darkness. But now, each day was a flash of color that leaped rebelliously out of the surrounding pallidity of people. Another secret frontier against the almost-forgotten. A fugitive shape from the scraps of society. A new name. All because of her...

But after the rabbit, I never saw her again. The empty space where she'd always sat during her lunch breaks yawned wider and more terribly than the obscurity of a black hole. And everything began to crumble. It took me a week to put together the pieces, and another to ask Greyson about it.

'That woman…' I trailed off. I realized I'd never had the courage to ask her name. 'The one with the paper creatures, the one whose home you…'

'Yeah, what about her?'

'What happened to her?'

He shrugged. 'Relocated.'

I realized I never saw any of the people whose residences we raided, after they were caught with any non-government-allocated possessions. I never thought much about it before. It wasn't my domain. Sadness, anger, desperation. All of these emotions were only to be expected. But the fear… the overwhelming fear was what I remembered the most. How it molded and stretched the face in the exact same way. A fear that surpassed simply getting told off, paying a fine, or having their relics taken away. What were they afraid of? And how were they being silenced?

I felt my throat tighten. 'Where?'

Another apathetic shrug, another dull-eyed stare. 'How am I supposed to know?'

He left me there, feeling like the scum of the earth.

*

Sometimes I liked to picture her in her new life, wherever she was. I liked to imagine that it was a better one, one where her work meant she was mostly outside.

Her skin, no longer pale under fluorescent lights, but golden from the gentle caress of sunlight. She closes those beautiful green eyes for a moment. Soaking up life like some magnificent tree with its branches outstretched and its leaves, full of whispered stories, tilted to catch the warmth of the sun.

I recalled her smile in my mind's eye each day so that I would never forget even a single ounce of its vibrancy. She's smiling now, in this brave new world of hers. Breathing in the air. Feeling its history. Making transitory sculptures out of leaves and twigs on her breaks, showing her new friends along with cascading laughter and a few murmured legends from the past, before letting the wind take them again. And even after her friends returned to sleek grayness after work, her memory would carry them safely to shore.

A promise, of more hues and shapes and stories to color tomorrow. A hope that it didn't all end with me. They were such little things, these paper creations. So minuscule in comparison to the daunting ubiquity and ruthless efficiency of the system. Her fleeting rebellions… they couldn't possibly change the world. But even if they spread only briefly, touched the hearts and dreams of a few janitors before all being wiped clean, this was enough. I wouldn't have traded it for the world.

'We don't need much, do we, Violet?' I whispered fondly to my little paper bird. Thumb, forefinger, flexing its little wings. It had taken me months to figure this one out. She'd taught me the rabbit, but the rest I had to do on my own.

I felt a tap on the shoulder and turned to face Grayson with a bundle of trash under one arm. 'What have you got there?' Something glistered briefly behind those usually dull eyes of his.

I handed it to him with a cordial shrug. 'See for yourself.'

Greyson cocked his head and squinted at the transfigured carton. Handled the thing carefully, almost scientifically between his fingers, before tossing it gently back to me. 'Okay, I'm stumped.'

'It's a milk carton, of course,' I shrugged again, this time with an almost melodramatically feigned apathy.

'That's not what I meant,' Greyson scoffed, though a slight eager irritation managed to tinge the edges of his voice.

'It's an animal. Or at least, it's folded in a way that's meant to look like one.'

'What kind?'

And for the first time, since the last time I had seen her, I allowed myself the ghost of a smile. Felt its warmth spread across my face, then down my neck. To my chest.

Remembering. 'A friend once told me it was called a penguin.'

'Penguin? Never heard of it.'

'It's a bird,' I continued, flapping its long, blade-like wings outwards with my thumb and forefinger as a small demonstration, 'and it flies underwater.'

Greyson's eyes widened. 'Impossible,' he chortled, then stopped short, his heavy brow furrowing in a mix of deep contemplation and wonder as he considered the logistics of such an otherworldly phenomena for a moment, before his face lit up and he was laughing again. 'Impossible!'

'There's no such thing.' I winked at him, then handed him the penguin again. 'Detritus. You know what to do.'

. . .

ABOUT THE AUTHORS

ALI SAID

Ali Said is a mixed-race, gay writer. Born in Dagenham, he went to school in the UAE before returning to London for university. He has since lived in places as diverse as New York and Cairo but is now back in south London. Ali's writing focuses on multicultural interactions and the many different ways in which we find our own paths. His stories have been listed for several prizes and he can be found on Twitter @AliSaidWrote.

CATHERINE RUDOLPH

Catherine Rudolph is a part-time writer and educator at the University of Cape Town. She recently completed her Master's in Creative Writing and wants to study further, looking at feminist and queer writings of the body. She struggles to define her work as 'fiction', it being so deeply rooted in her own experience, but she would like to make collaborative fiction one day. Teaching and learning from her students are her other joys.

DEBORAH GREEN

Deborah Green writes from the world of sex work, of the masks we wear, even when naked. Working in strip clubs for many years has revealed the human condition to her. Deborah teaches yoga and meditation in India, Ibiza and Manchester. She has organised writing retreats in the UK and abroad, recently with an emphasis on supporting voices from sex work. She is nomadic by nature, with roots in the north-west of England.

FERNANDO A. TORRES

Fernando A. Torres is a short-story writer, freelance journalist, musician and poet, currently performing around the San Francisco Bay Area and contributing to various San Francisco Bay Area media outlets about community, art and culture including La Opinión de la Bahía, Fresno's Radio Bilingue, and *El Tecolote* San Francisco's Latino bilingual newspaper. He is also a non-pay associate editor and US correspondent for the Latin American web magazine *Dilemas.cl* and editor of the blog magazine *LatinOpen*.

Dedicated to Chicano actor, comedian & 'stutter' poet José Antonio Burciaga (RIP).

KIKI GONGLEWSKI

Kiki Gonglewski, a sophomore at Columbia University, is a storyteller avidly exploring different media. Writing has been a lifelong love, and she hopes she can pay the rent with it someday! When she is not catching up on classes or working on making movies, writing, or an art project, Kiki spends her time daydreaming and drawing up plans for intergalactic travel in some obscure corner of Butler library. She is a large fan of movies, Bradbury novels, Korean Barbeque, all things stars, and long afternoon naps.

MICHAEL HARRIS COHEN

Michael Harris Cohen has work published or forthcoming in various magazines and anthologies including *Black Candies*, *The Dark*, Catapult's *Tiny Crimes*, the *Exposition Review* and *Conjunctions*. He is the winner of the Modern Grimmoire Literary Prize, a Fulbright grant for literary translation and fellowships from The Djerassi Foundation, OMI International Arts Center, Jentel, and the Künstlerdorf Schöppingen Foundation. He lives with his wife and daughters in Sofia and teaches in the department of Literature and Theatre at the American University in Bulgaria.

MITRA TEYMOORIAN

Mitra Teymoorian was born in Tehran in 1968. She studied painting in high school and then she studied photography, and has taught photography. For more than two decades, she has enjoyed travelling and capturing life moments. Once she turned forty years old, she found out that writing was her true passion. She has also written many short and long stories, which are waiting to be published.

MUBANGA KALIMAMUKWENTO

Mubanga Kalimamukwento is a Zambian writer and lawyer; her first novel, *The Mourning Bird* (Jacana), won the Dinaane Debut Fiction Award in 2019. The same year, she won the Kalemba Short Story Prize and was shortlisted for the Bristol Short Story Prize. She's been published in journals in Zambia, Namibia, Nigeria, Canada, Australia, France, the UK and the USA. Mubanga is an alumna of the Hubert H. Humphrey (Fulbright) Fellowship and the Young African Leaders Initiative. She's a current MFA candidate at Hamline University where she received the Writer of Colour Merit Scholarship. She lives in Minnesota, with her husband and two children.

NATHAN ALLING LONG

Nathan Alling Long's work appears in over 100 publications, including *Tin House, Glimmer Train, Story Quarterly* and *The Sun*. His stories have won international contests and been nominated three times for the Pushcart Prize. His collection of fifty short fictions, *The Origin of Doubt* (Press 53), was a finalist for the Lambda Literary Award, and his second manuscript was a finalist for the Hudson Book Manuscript Prize and the Iowa Fiction Award. A recipient of a Mellon Foundation grant and a Truman Capote literary fellowship, Nathan lives in Philadelphia and teaches creative writing at Stockton University.

SELMA CARVALHO

Selma Carvalho is a prize-winning British Asian writer and author of three non-fiction books documenting the Goan presence is colonial East Africa. Her poetry and fiction have been widely published. She has been listed or placed in numerous contests including by Mslexia, Fish, Bath, Brighton and London Short Story. She won the Leicester Writes Short Story Prize 2018. Her collection of short stories was longlisted for the SI Leeds Literary Prize.

STEPHANIE WILDERSPIN

Stephanie Wilderspin grew up in Essex, raised by the stereotype of a single mother on benefits. She graduated with a degree in American Literature with Creative Writing from the University of East Anglia, and currently works as a researcher for a prominent TV broadcaster. Stephanie's writing often explores social issues with a focus on gender, sexuality, class, and mental illness. She enjoys finding unorthodox ways to explore serious issues, by playing with format and structure and utilising comedy to navigate difficult topics to make her writing more relatable, all while retaining a poignant message at its core.

TIMI ODUESO

Timi Odueso is a Nigerian undergraduate student who will read anything, anything other than his law books. He is the winner of the 2019 Sevhage Nonfiction Prize and a Literary Critic Fellow at Wawa Book Review. His fiction has been published or is upcoming in *On the Premises*, *The Single Story Foundation*, the *US Embassy Missions* and *McSweeney's Quarterly Concern*, amongst others.

ACKNOWLEDGEMENTS

In late 2019 we launched our first ever short-story competition to support new and emerging writers of short-form fiction and non-fiction. We put out an open call for writers to send us their response to the chosen theme of The Censor. We were overwhelmed by the response from all over the world and impressed by the high quality of writing. We have had the pleasure to read so many ingenious and surprising short stories from a diverse selection of writers.

Thank you to our external judges Coco Khan and Amyra Leon who helped us select the final twelve stories for this anthology.

We would also like to say a big thank you to the huge team of readers whose thoughts and expertise helped us to narrow down all the entries in the early stages of the competition. Thank you to:

Anita Goveas, Anna Livia Ryan, Carmina Bernhardt, Catriona Knox, Charlotte Forfieh, Christopher Newlove Horton, Claire Blakemore, Emily Ford, Erika Banerji, Graeme Williams, Jupiter Jones, Karen Clarke, Katie Baldock, Laurane Marchive, L M Dillsworth, Lillian Weber, Lou Kramskoy, Louise Hare, Madi Maxwell-Libby, Mandy Rabin, Mari Lawton, Miranda Miller, Natasha Baddeley, Natasha Cutler, Nise McCulloch, Patrick Towey, Roanne O'Neil, Sabrina Richmond, Satu Hämeenaho-Fox, Simon Miller, Wendy Lothian and Zoë Aubugeau-Williams.

Above all, thank you to the writers from all around the world for telling their stories and sharing them with us.